A Flash of Fireflies

AISHA BUSHBY

Farshore

First published in Great Britain in 2022 by Farshore

An imprint of HarperCollins*Publishers*
1 London Bridge Street, London SE1 9GF

farshore.co.uk

HarperCollins*Publishers*
1st Floor, Watermarque Building,
Ringsend Road, Dublin 4, Ireland

A CIP catalogue record of this title is available from the British Library

ISBN 978 0 7555 0064 2
Printed and bound in the UK using 100% renewable electricity at
CPI Group (UK) Ltd
1

Typeset by Avon DataSet Ltd, Alcester, Warwickshire

MIX
Paper from
responsible sources
FSC™ C007454

ONCE UPON A TIME...

There was a girl who lived in a desert home with her parents. Her favourite thing to do on a hot summer's day was to count the ants that crawled along her courtyard garden, one by one, until they disappeared into a crack in the wall of her concrete home. While she counted, she sang a song:

The ants go marching one by one
Hurrah, hurrah
The ants go marching one by one
Hurrah, hurrah
The ants go marching one by one
The little one stops to suck his thumb
And they all march down to the ground
For to get out of the rain
Boom, boom, boom

At the last line she would clap three times, before moving on to the next verse. Sometimes she would do this for hours and hours, until the sun disappeared and she could no longer see the ants. Until the winds arrived and she was called inside for fear of catching a cold.

One day, while the girl was counting, a different sort of creature landed in front of her: a firefly, followed by a second and a third. They began to sing the song along with her, until she found herself marching after them. They formed a crack in the wall just like the ones she had watched the ants crawl through and, as it grew larger and larger, she followed them into it.

Only the girl and the fireflies knew what lay in the crack beyond the wall, and she returned home soon after, filled with stories of quests and whispering voices in a magical forest. Her parents entertained her tales because, after all, children have wild imaginations. But neither of them believed the stories, because they sounded like something out of a fairy tale.

Not long after, the girl's stories turned to nightmares. She spoke of three fireflies that visited her night after night, and each time they scratch, scratch, scratched at her skin. Her parents grew worried, because they saw the marks on her hands, like ink spots on a map.

And so they told her to let them know whenever the fireflies arrived; they even sought help from those with experience in such matters. And it worked. The spell was broken and the fireflies no longer bothered the child.

Soon after, life carried on, and the girl's memories faded like the scratches on her skin. She forgot about the ants and the fireflies, and she played games of a different sort. Games that gave her grazed knees and arms, but no scratches on her hands for her parents to worry about.

One day, the girl's life changed, as sudden as a rain cloud arriving on a sunny day.

And the past her parents had worked so hard to bury dug itself back out, ready to claim her again.

CHAPTER 1

I cling on to Dad the hardest, mainly because I know he's the weaker link.

'Please, please, *please* can I stay with you?' I ask.

Mama sighs impatiently. 'We've been over this, ya elbi, you'll only be without us for a few weeks. It's going to be manic here, and very boring for you with a house full of boxes. We want you to get settled before you start school in September.'

'I can't believe you expect me to go live with a stranger in a whole new country,' I say accusingly, still hugging Dad, who hasn't tried to let go yet either. He's gone completely silent.

I can practically hear Mama roll her eyes. 'Your aunt raised your father from when he was a young child right up until he left to travel. She's as much a part of our

family as you. Honestly, Hazel –'

'So what? Should I call her Mama too?' I ask, scrunching up my face. I'm not sure I'm ready to be alone with my great-aunt all summer.

'If you like, then yes.' Mama starts to laugh now, letting out a snort. 'It'd give me a bit of a break. Maybe I can travel more? Oh, how about Nepal? I've always wanted to go there!'

I ignore Mama because she's being silly, and finally pull away from Dad, looking up into his brown-green eyes. His moustache twitches and I know I'm about to break his resolve. I can see it in his eyes, the way he sniffs.

'Dad, don't make meanie Mama send me away, please?'

Dad sighs the sigh I know means he's about to give me bad news. 'We'll be there with you as soon as you know it, and we'll be one big, happy family in England. We all agreed to it together, didn't we?'

'*I* didn't agree to it,' I protest. 'You did.'

'Exactly,' Dad says, as if I've proven his point. 'So it's not your mother's fault.'

'Oh yes, it is,' Mama says in a croaky voice, going full-on hyper mode. 'It's all my fault, for I'm the jinni that's stealing you away from your home.' She's creeping around us now, and a few people turn to look, a little alarmed.

'Stop it, Mama,' I say, like a parent scolding their child, aware of the strange looks we're getting. But I can't help but break into a smile now, as Mama lets out an evil cackle.

The tannoy makes a sound then, and I hear a robotic voice call my flight number and gate. It makes my stomach flip and whirl and I realise it's happening. It's *really* happening. I'm about to get on a plane by myself and move to England. My parents will be joining me at the end of the summer, but I wish they were coming now.

A wave of people start heading towards the security machines, like a school of fish moving as one. I can feel myself being pulled towards them, and away from my parents and home.

'Hazel Al-Otaibi?' an unfamiliar voice says my name. The surname belongs to Mama's family, because Dad doesn't really have a relationship with his parents.

When I turn, I see an air steward standing a few paces away. He has shiny black hair and friendly eyes. His smile is bright, like a Barbie doll's, and he's standing completely still and poised, waiting patiently.

'That's right,' says Dad, confirming my name for me.

The air steward introduces himself as Mohammed, but says I can call him Mo.

Suddenly, Mama grabs my hand, firm, and I can see in her eyes that she's as sad about being separated as I am. Even if it's only for a little while.

'It won't be long, all right?' Mama says, and I can see her eyes shining with tears.

I nod, sniffing, and pull her in for another hug, taking in her coffee-scented smell. Dad hands me my suitcase and says goodbye, his voice shaking.

I turn to Mo.

He smiles kindly. 'Don't worry. I'll be here with you the whole way.'

After we make it past security (they made me walk through in my socks which felt strange), Mo takes me to a private waiting room, and it's not long until we're on the flight. We're one of the first to enter – there are only a few other people on board, mostly staff.

'When you travel as an unaccompanied minor,' Mo explains, 'you get the VIP treatment.'

He's not wrong. I walk through first class, which has these fancy seats that fold back into beds, but Mo stops me short.

'You're in luck,' he says. 'We have a spare seat, so we've upgraded you!'

'Really?' I say, peering at the plush loungers.

Mo nods. 'Right here, near the cabin, so I can keep an eye on you.' He leads me to my seat and shows me a little curtain I can pull which basically makes it my very own den. He says I can have as many fizzy drinks as I want and second helpings of dessert. Even though today is scary, and my whole world is turning around, it's fun too.

The air-conditioning turns on and the cool breeze calms me a little, as does the sound of it. It's what I listen to every night before falling asleep.

I find my favourite TV show on the screen and spend most of the flight watching that. I've already seen every episode but it's nice to have some familiarity. After food is served (pizza and chips, with chocolate cake!), I fall in and out of sleep like a cat, and curl up like one too. Mo keeps an eye on me, but gives me space, which I appreciate. I think he knows what a big deal this move is.

Somehow, up in the air, it's like the world is on pause, and I forget about meeting my great-aunt. I forget about staying with her alone all summer, and starting a new school, and everything else that's going on.

Instead, I think of my family in Kuwait. Mama has two sisters: one in America, the other in Singapore. She has a brother too, who's closer to my age than hers. He's about to start university in England, and Mama would be the last one of her family in Kuwait. So she found a new job and decided we would move to England too, where Dad's from.

It was nice growing up with my cousins around all the time; not as nice when they all left. Still, I suppose it's our turn now.

The seat belt sign comes on, and the captain announces that we're about to descend. I look out of the window and see a patchwork quilt of fields in green, orange and yellow. They're connected by roads that look like stitches, and houses that resemble beads. It's beautiful.

I feel a jolt, and the plane lowers, ready to land. Suddenly, the world and my future come whizzing towards me.

CHAPTER 2

Fridays used to be my favourite day of the week.

It's the first day of the weekend in Kuwait, so my cousins, aunts and uncles would organise a big lunch with my grandparents. We would spend the whole day eating, talking and playing. Usually my cousins and I would practise a play to perform in the evening, and Mama's brother would come up with a musical beat on his drums to tap, tap, tap with his hands.

As the eldest cousin, I was always the director, but Mama said I can get too bossy, and I needed to let my next oldest cousin Omar (who is exactly seven months and four days younger than me) take the lead sometimes.

Except Omar was always annoying and disorganised, so we would argue and wrestle until our mamas had to pull us apart. We could never stay mad at each for long, though, because we were a team: me, Omar, his baby sister (who just cried most of the time) and our other cousins Amal and Adel.

I once asked Mama and Dad why I didn't have a sibling like the others. They explained that I was a special gift, and that I was enough to fill their whole hearts. It never mattered that I was an only child because, with my cousins around every weekend, I never felt lonely.

We would do our homework together and go to the theme park and beach and carry as many sweets as we could hold in our hands during Gargee'an (which is kind of like Halloween, without the monsters).

But then, one day, while I was getting ready for another Friday gathering, I heard my parents' hushed voices down the hall.

'Are you *sure?*' I could hear Mama say, her voice all wobbly. 'But he was fine . . .'

'I'm so sorry, love,' said Dad, his voice soft like that time I was too scared to get my jab at the doctor's.

It took me a while to realise that my grandfather had passed away. And somehow I knew, even then, that things were going to change.

My grandmother passed away a year after and our family thread loosened like an old piece of well-worn clothing. Omar's parents decided to move them to America, and Amal and Adel's baba got a job in Singapore.

Soon, it was just Mama and Dad, me and my uncle. I missed seeing Omar every week, and if I could I'd have let him be director every Friday, just to have them all back again.

Then it was our turn. When Mama and Dad told me we were moving to England, they explained we even had a house to stay in, living with Dad's aunt, who had enough room for all of us.

'It's like the gingerbread house from the stories I used to tell you at bedtime!' Dad had said enthusiastically. 'It looks just the same.'

I was sad about the move at first. But every day Mama and Dad told me different things about England – the other half of where I'm from. It was when they said it had loads of insects to discover that I started to come round to the idea. Ever since I used to count ants out in our courtyard, I've loved bugs and try to find them wherever I go.

And when they told me there could be snow, and I'd need to wear a coat in the winter, and we'd visit Omar and his family in the holidays, I started to get even a little bit excited about the thought of living somewhere new.

After all, even though the fabric of our family had loosened, we were still one and the same, and we would find each other again and again and again.

CHAPTER 3

Home to me is sand and sea – I can taste it in the air, feel it seep down my throat and into my veins. It hugs my insides in its warm embrace. England is different. It gives me a strange new feeling I can barely contain in my bones.

As I step off the plane and down the steep metal stairs on to the airport tarmac, I feel a chill in the air. It's the middle of July but the sky is filled with grey clouds and there's a breeze that whips at my face, pulling me along the concourse.

It carries with it the smell of rubber and oil, but beyond that, beneath the smokiness of plane engines, is pine and grass.

As we enter the airport, Mo chats about the secret passages, and how to get to them, which I only half listen to even though it's something I'd usually find interesting.

The other half of my brain is pure panic. It sort of feels like I'm underwater, and he's speaking in this muffled voice I can barely hear. Everyone moves past me in slow motion, and the walk to pick up my suitcase feels endless.

As we watch the bags go round and round the conveyor belt, I start to feel a little sick, like I'm the one being spun around. I almost hope I'll never find mine, so I can stand here in the limbo between worlds and never have to enter my new life. But then I see it: the bright yellow suitcase my parents insisted on me taking so I could find it more easily.

'Ah, there it is!' says Mo, stepping forward to grab it for me. As he struggles to take hold of the handle, jogging a little to keep up, I swear I see them: three fireflies, scuttling around the side of the suitcase, one trying to crawl through a gap in the zip, the other two pulling at a loose thread at the seams.

My heart leaps and I jump back, almost tripping over someone else's luggage. I thought I had left the fireflies in my past. But they're here, and I can feel the same tingling sensation in my hands that I always do when they arrive. How can they have followed me here, halfway across the world?

You might think fireflies are bright, glowing creatures, but that's only at night. During the day they look a bit like beetles, with black wings and red faces. It's as if they wear masks to disguise their true selves, only revealing their real identity at night. A group of them, like the ones I think I see flitting around my suitcase, are called a light posse, or a sparkle. But I like to think of them as a flash, like lightning.

The fireflies started arriving when I was nine, when my grandfather passed away and everyone was sad all the time. At first, we were friends. They would meet me in the scorching courtyard of my family home, where I was busy counting a colony of ants, and slowly, they would draw me away to adventures new.

A tree, filled with fruit, that we climbed and climbed to the very top.

'Pluck the biggest fruit,' the fireflies would whisper in my ear, a secret. 'Bring it down for us,' they would hiss.

And so I did.

But the more I fed them, the hungrier they became.

And soon one tree became two, became four, became a forest.

I tried to ignore them, for a time, but they would scratch, scratch, scratch at my skin, making it itch and tingle. And, when I eventually gave in, they would whisk me off on my next adventure.

Adventures sound rather exciting, I know. Most stories will tell you to seek them. But the sorts of adventures I went on were bothersome, repetitive and exhausting.

And so I started to fear the fireflies' next arrival. I dreaded it, like a storm cloud waiting to drop rain on me when I least expected it.

Eventually, my parents took me to a doctor who explained that the fireflies seemed to arrive when I was feeling anxious or worried, and that I shouldn't listen to their demands. It was difficult, at first, but with the help of Mama and Dad, they eventually went away.

Until now.

Mo finally heaves my suitcase with force off the conveyor belt.

'It's heavy!' he says, with an awkward chuckle. 'What have you got in there, a dead body?' He quickly realises that's not the most appropriate thing to say to a 12-year-old, but I laugh and his face relaxes a little.

When I look back at the suitcase, the fireflies are gone and I feel like I can breathe again.

'What do we do now?' I ask Mo. It's the first time I've said anything since we stepped off the plane, even though I usually find it *hard* to *stop* speaking. I think it's the fireflies – I'm itching to get far away from them, lose them somewhere before they call for me again.

'Now,' Mo explains. 'We walk through those doors and try to spot your aunt in the crowd of people.'

'Great-aunt,' I correct him, and then explain what one of those is. 'So she's probably older than you're expecting.'

Mo laughs at that for some reason and then he pushes my luggage trolley for me, and I hurry alongside him.

As the double doors open for us automatically, the cacophony of voices greeting one another blend into one, loud, happy song.

I expect to wait a while, but it turns out that spotting my great-aunt is easier than I had expected.

'There she is!' Mo declares, pointing at a woman I had only seen in photos. She's sandwiched between dozens of people, but she stands out like a queen ant amidst her colony.

'Oh yeah,' I say, my mouth suddenly dry, my chest tight. She's holding a sign up with my name, *Hazel Al-Otaibi*, written on it in calligraphy that looks as if it belongs in an old book. But that's not the only thing that seems as if it's from the past. She has her hair tied up into a neat bun, with a pearl clasp at one side, and she's wearing a ruffled shirt and red velvet trousers, even though everyone else is in jeans and T-shirts. If I didn't know any better, I'd think she was a time traveller, stuck in the wrong age, but Dad explained that she's eccentric, which is a fancy way of saying different.

Looking at her now, I see Dad in her eyes as they search for me, and her white skin that would burn in the Kuwaiti sun. I'm so used to seeing Mama's family, where everyone looks like a slightly different slice of the same cake. Mama's features weave themselves through me in my nose and lips and brown skin. But this is the first time I've seen a different piece of Dad.

We don't talk much about his parents: they decided that bringing up a kid wasn't the job for them and left it up to my great-aunt, his mother's older sister, to raise him. Dad loves my great-aunt Hazel with his whole heart – so much so he even named me after her. Except, when we first spoke on the phone, she told me to call her 'Grant' because it sounds like a mix-up of 'great' and 'aunt'. She seemed really pleased when she thought of it, as if giving me our name was a gift.

When Grant sees me, she recognises me at once. Her smile, accented with wrinkles at the corner of her lips, grows larger, and she nods, before pulling the sign down.

Grant crouches so she's my height, as Mo hands me over to her – two strangers, passing me between them.

'Hello, Hazel,' she says, and if I stare into her eyes I can almost pretend I'm talking to Dad. So I do, as I nod back and say: 'Hello, Grant.'

CHAPTER 4

The journey to Grant's house is strange. Like her clothes, Grant's car is old, and it bounces a lot, juddering around as she drives. I can feel my teeth and bones rattle as we move along the road, and the engine is so loud I struggle to hear whenever she talks to me. I awkwardly keep asking her to repeat herself, before giving up and nodding my head politely.

It's almost 6 p.m., a whole ten hours since I said goodbye to my parents at the airport in Kuwait. And in that time everything has changed. It feels like I've entered a new world, a new dimension, but also, with Grant, like I've stepped back in time.

We stop at a service station to get some food, and it's nice to feel my bones return to their normal places in my body – nice for the humming to stop. We step into a brightly lit food hall with lots of different cuisines.

'I'm having noodles,' Grant says, walking over to a stall with the shortest queue. 'What about you?'

There's fast food, but right now I want something that reminds me of home, even if only a little. The noodle stall, I notice, has rice and chicken, and even though I don't recognise the sauce, that's good enough for me. So I do the same.

When we sit down I watch the odd assortment of people that have gathered here. There are people in business suits, eating alone, scanning their phones. A tired-looking couple who stare listlessly at their coffees. And Grant and I. She doesn't fit in here either. In fact, she stands out even more than she did at the airport, which is why the question I ask tumbles out of my mouth before I can stop it.

'Are you a time traveller?' It might sound silly, but whenever Dad talks about his childhood he always mentions things that seem as if they belong in a world from one hundred years ago, and I'm fairly certain he's not *that* old. Instead of video games, he played croquet as a child, and he still carries a pocket watch that Grant gave him for his thirteenth birthday.

Grant laughs at this, and that's another thing I realise she shares with Dad.

'I wish,' she says, slurping up her noodles with a pair of chopsticks while I pick at my rice with a fork. I don't feel hungry now. The lights are too bright and ahead of me a neon sign for a sweet shop keeps flickering, making my eyes twitch. There's too much going on for me to even think about eating. 'Wouldn't it be fun? I think I'd like to see a dinosaur if I could. But unfortunately, no, I'm not a time traveller. I just like to collect old things.' She shrugs. 'Clothes, antiques . . . But I also *love* new books and television shows.'

Somehow I can't imagine Grant watching TV. Or maybe she does but everything is in black and white.

'I suppose that's sort of like time travelling,' I say. 'Collecting old things.'

Grant stops eating for a moment and peers at me with a strange look on her face.

'I'd never thought about it that way, but I suppose you're right.'

After we've eaten we get back into the bouncy car and drive for a few more hours. I close my eyes and try to imagine I'm in the car on the way home with Dad and Mama, and we're going to pull up at our concrete house with its dusty white gate, instead of a tiny village in the middle of England.

Except, a few hours later – after I drift into dreams of my old and new world jumbling together like clothes in a washer – the car pulls off the main road and I find myself in a tiny village in the middle of England. The roads are windy here, with no pavements, and all of the buildings are made from limestone, Grant explains. Now that the roads are a bit slower, the engine hum quietens, so I can hear what she's saying. Then she pulls up on to a gravelly road and drives a few metres along.

On either side of us are tall hedges, blocking the road and neighbours from view, and up ahead is a cottage with four windows and a door, shining beneath the moonlight. It has smoke billowing from a chimney. We step out of the car and the only sounds I can hear is the gravel beneath our feet, the slam of our car doors, and Grant's keys jangling as she locks up.

From somewhere in the distance is the sound of running water, like a tap. But I realise it must be a stream.

It's hard to see anything as we approach the front door; and as Grant opens it, letting me go in first, even harder to see when we get inside. She turns on a light, but everything is dim, gloomy, like she'd only lit a candle instead.

'Energy-saving,' Grant explains. 'Takes time for them to brighten up. But we can do a proper tour tomorrow. For now, shoes off, hands washed, and time for bed.'

She says this cheerily, but there's a sternness in her voice too, like she expects to be listened to. I step on to the welcome mat, too scared to go any further through the threshold of her home, as Grant flits around. She takes my shoes and puts them in a cupboard, locks up the front door and pulls a velvet curtain over it, and then turns back to me and peers at my suitcase.

'Do you think you can manage that on your own? You're just at the top of the stairs.'

'I think so,' I say, carrying the weight of the suitcase alone. It reminds me of all the things I've had to do on my own today, and though it's scary, I'm proud of myself too.

Dad's old bedroom – which is mine now, I guess – is small. There's just room for a bed, table, wardrobe and desk all squished together.

'Tuck your suitcase under your bed for now, but tomorrow you'll need to empty it as there's no room for mess in here,' Grant continues, seemingly unfazed by the fact that I've only said three words since we entered the house.

As she continues to give instructions – where the toilet is, when we'll have breakfast and what time I'll be going to bed – I realise I really *have* stepped into a different world. It's not just that England is different, but Grant's house is too.

After she leaves me to settle, I change quickly and crawl into bed. I close my eyes and try to carry on with my fantasy: after the car journey home with Dad and Mama, I'm tucked into my own bed. But I can't because there are no sounds from the whooshing air-conditioning, and the bed sheets are scratchy, the duvet heavy and the pillow too plump.

It finally hits me that this *is* my new home. Not just for the summer, but after that too, when Mama and Dad arrive.

If they arrive. The thought surprises me, the seed of it buried deep. Dad's parents were meant to drop him off with Grant for just a couple of weeks. But those weeks turned to months, turned to years. What if the same happens to me?

Grant's room is just down the hall, and Mama and Dad's room is meant to be up in the attic. Grant converted it especially for them.

I try to blink back the tears that come, but I can't. So instead I look up at the ceiling and try to transport myself back to my real home a different way. I rewind the entire day and imagine the plane flying backwards through the stars, taking me back to Kuwait.

Then three very *real* stars start glowing above my head, spinning in circles. I sit up and realise that they're not stars at all, but fireflies.

They fly through a gap between the wardrobe doors and I pull the covers off myself and crawl across the room like a spider, peering through after them. I'm sure it's the fireflies from before, because my chest feels tight and my hands feel tingly like they did at the airport. The only relief comes from following them, even as my brain is screaming at me not to.

I can't see anything, so I pull the wardrobe door open

with a creak. I expect to be met by the fireflies crawling around and some old clothes. Instead, I find a cluster of leaves and branches, and a gap at the back of the wardrobe, just big enough for me to climb through. The fireflies perch on leaves, waiting, before they disappear through the dark, gaping hole. I hesitate for a moment, knowing there's no turning back once I go after them. But if I don't go, and get back into bed instead, they'll scratch scratch scratch at my skin until they draw blood.

So, knowing I don't really have a choice in this strange new country on my own, I follow.

CHAPTER 5

My parents used to tell me bedtime stories; the ones they were told when they were young. Mama has this story about sea witches who sail to different islands and share their magic; it's set in the Middle East, where she's from, with rocs and jinn and all sorts of magical creatures.

Dad would tell me the story of Hansel and Gretel and how they had to leave their home. I guess it's because that's what happened to him: he followed a breadcrumb trail all the way to Grant. In his version of the story the children find a lovely gingerbread home with a kindly witch, who feeds them all the food they could want until they grow older and stronger. He ended his story with 'happily ever after', but I'm not so sure any more that fairy tales do have happy endings.

It takes me a while of shuffling through the wardrobe to realise I've arrived halfway up a tree. I recognise it at once, as familiar as my bed at home, from all those other times I've followed the fireflies. Except it's been a while now. Protruding from the tree's bark are long red hairs, not quite as thick as an animal's, but soft enough to stroke. I feel a cat-like purring beneath my palms when I do, and the trunk shivers, rolling its wooden knots up and down in a wave. It's my only comfort in the firefly forest, which is what I've come to call this place.

With just the moonlight to break up the gloom, I shuffle around the tree's limb-like branches to inspect my surroundings. It responds to my movements, like I'm leading us in a dance. Closer up I can see it has cuts and grazes oozing blood instead of sap, the way my hands used to when the fireflies scratch, scratch, scratched.

Come down. Come down. Come down, three silky voices request. An echo. They start as a whisper but grow louder each time, make my skin break out in bumps and the hairs on the back of my neck stand on end. The hairs on the tree trunk and branches are on end too, like they feel the same way I do. The whispers flow through my bloodstream, drumming in my head, making my teeth chatter.

For the first time, I peer through some leaves below and I can see the fireflies through them, floating above wet grass. They're bigger here, the size of my hand, and I can see their beady eyes watch me, their antennae reaching. As I climb down, slowly and carefully, the tree limbs aid me, lowering a little to bridge the gap, making sure I don't slip. The trees have always looked out for me, even as I collected the fruits of their labour for the fireflies.

Finally, I feel my bare feet on the grass. It's cold and wet, reminding me that in spite of the trees and their loyalty to me, this ever-moving forest belongs to the fireflies. The ground rumbles gently, and makes a sound like faint snoring. The trees' life source exists in its roots, beneath the ground, and the fireflies have trapped them here. Like me.

Pluck the fruit. Pluck the fruit. Pluck the fruit, the fireflies demand, surrounding me now. It's a request they made many times before, years ago, and I never knew how many pieces would satisfy them. Once it was six – two for each of them, but on one of the worst times they wanted 444. I piled up each piece of fruit until it towered over me like a mountain. It took hours, and I scoured the entire periphery of the forest, worried I would run out of fruit to pluck and be stuck there forever.

Because that's the thing – I'm never allowed to return home unless I complete the fireflies' quest.

And so I do.

Though I've grown older since I was last here, the firefly

forest is exactly the same. So it doesn't take long for me to fall into my familiar routine.

I find the first apple – red and juicy – at the base of the tree I've just climbed down. It lifts up its roots to help me reach it. There's a second one not far away, half hidden in the grass. Like the fireflies, the apples too are bigger here than they are in the normal world, a single leaf protruding from their stems. The third and fourth hang low on branches, and the fifth and sixth require some climbing. As I pluck and pluck I hear the fireflies' requests for, *More. More. More*, buzzing through the air.

Time here is measured in fruit. Except I've never seen the fireflies eat any of it, so I don't know what they want with it. They just hover while I pick and pluck and dig and pile. I'm tired from all the travelling and emotions about everything changing. In one day I've been to Kuwait and England and the firefly forest and all I want is to sleep and dream. But I know I can't leave until I'm done.

By the thirtieth piece of fruit plucked, my insides start to squirm as panic takes over and I grit my teeth, tears spilling down my face. Ten pieces of fruit later, the fireflies release me. And I do something I've never done before: I pluck one more piece of fruit for myself, and hide it in the folds of my dressing gown. Perhaps if I study it later then I can understand why they want it so much.

The forest darkens, the fireflies have gone, and when

I blink there are wardrobe doors ahead, waiting for me to open them. I stumble out and place the apple on my bedside table before removing my dressing gown and crawling back into bed.

CHAPTER 6

Waking up in someone else's house is strange. As you lie there, eyes closed, you forget for a moment where you are. The mattress feels different, as do the pillows and cover. Then you notice the sounds are different too, as are the smells.

In Kuwait the mornings were quiet. My parents like to sleep in, so I often spent hours awake playing while I waited for them. I loved mornings because they were my grown-up-free time, but here it's different.

I can hear Grant in the kitchen now. There's the sound of water boiling, followed by clattering pans that make my teeth hurt. I squeeze my eyes shut, hoping for a moment that this simple act will transport me back home. I even sit there and imagine that when I next open them I'll see my bedroom, with my dressing table covered in stuffed toys and nail varnish.

But when I open my eyes again I don't see any of that, just the wooden bedroom door in front of me, and a bedside table to my left with an apple on it. When I see it, I remember the events of the night before: the purring trees and whispering fireflies; I remember all the apples I picked and the one sitting here that I stole. It's the first time I've brought something back from the firefly forest, and it's odd to see it here in this world.

'Breakfast!' Grant calls, her voice closer than I expect it to be. I realise she must have walked to the bottom of the stairs to tell me. I don't know whether she wants me to yell back, so I just put my dressing gown on, slide my feet into my slippers and rush downstairs.

In the daylight, I get the chance to see Grant's house properly. There's mismatched wallpaper and patterned carpets. There are lots of tables in the hall with random objects on them like a bowl of dried fruit, a teapot and some binoculars. There are photos too: of Grant and Dad, and Grant and a woman I don't recognise. The woman crops up a lot, with the two of them standing together in front of places I do recognise, like the pyramids and the Taj Mahal and Eiffel Tower. In between the photos are paintings of the sea and sky. It feels like walking through a museum – I'm not sure if I'm allowed to touch anything.

The stairs creak and the curtains flutter as a soft breeze

comes in through them. Dad's room – or mine now, I have to keep reminding myself – is at the top of the stairs, with a bathroom diagonally across from it. To the right of the bottom of the stairs is a long living room split in half with an arch. There are sofas on one side, and a bookcase and desk on the other. To the left of the stairs is the kitchen.

I follow the sounds to where Grant is standing in front of her stove, with a ladle in hand and two plates next to her on the counter. Each plate holds a slice of bread cut into strips. On the plates are egg cups that look like frogs, and she serves us each an egg, before carrying hers to the table.

'Here you go,' Grant says, nodding at my breakfast on the counter while she carries hers to the table.

I smile at her and grab my breakfast too, sitting across from her. I'm not really sure what to do with the egg – I've never had this before. But I watch as she taps hers with a teaspoon and picks off the top, adding salt and pepper before dipping a piece of bread in. I copy her, though I make a big mess of it, and I swear I see her glance at me with an amused expression on her face, but she says nothing.

We eat in silence for a while, the only sound is our chewing, the clearing of throats, or Grant sipping her coffee. The egg tastes a bit too peppery and slimy, and really I want to spit it out, but I swallow it down, hoping the next bite will be easier. I pour myself some orange juice from the jug on the table and swing my legs, feeling more and more awkward. I don't know whether I'm supposed to wait for her to speak first, seeing as it's her house.

Then, she finally asks, 'How did you sleep?'

I chew over her words. 'Erm, I slept on my back, I think. I was finding it hard to breathe sleeping on my belly like usual.'

Grant looks at me, confused for a moment, before laughing. 'Oh, no, I meant did you sleep well?'

I'm not sure how to answer that. Besides the visit from the fireflies – which kept me up later than I would have liked – I slept for a long time. But I still feel tired now.

I nod, because I think that's what Grant wants me to do, and say, 'Yes, thank you!'

She seems pleased.

'Well, eat up. I'll give you a quick tour of the house and then you're free to do as you please until lunch.' She walks over to her fridge to return the jug of orange juice. A tiny chalkboard has a list of tasks written out for the day.

Saturday
9 a.m. Breakfast
10 a.m. Weed garden
11 a.m. Plant seeds
12 p.m. Prepare lunch, read
1 p.m. Lunch

I'm not really sure if these chores are for me, or Grant, or both of us.

'Oh,' Grant laughs, when I ask. 'They're for me, apart from mealtimes. But you're welcome to join me if you like. Though I'll be honest, weeding the garden isn't much fun . . .'

After that, Grant goes over *my* schedule, which is busier than hers. I'll be attending summer school three days a week, which I already knew but had sort of ignored until now. Mama said it would be a good way to 'settle in and keep busy', and Dad said he made his 'best friends' at that very same school a whole thirty years ago.

The mornings are for lessons, and in the afternoons we get to work on our projects, or read, or use the school equipment. It all sounds fine, I guess, but what I didn't realise is that one of the days I'd be attending summer school would be on a Friday.

Back home, the weekends are on a Friday and Saturday, so it's weird to be switching to Saturday and Sunday here in England. But at least I have one more day after this one before I need to meet new people . . .

I'm just finishing up my last strip of bread when I feel something furry brush up against my leg.

I glance down to see a white creature with big ears lollop along the floor. I squeal, pulling my legs up to the seat of my chair before leaning forward to find out what it is.

Grant turns, looking startled, before glancing down to the creature. Her face lights up.

'Hello, Amélie,' Grant says, bending down to stroke it. She riffles through the fridge and pulls out some celery sticks. I can see now that it's a rabbit, but I have no idea why it's here, inside, and why Grant is feeding it. She looks up at me. 'Sorry, I forgot to tell you – this is Amélie, my house rabbit.'

'House rabbit,' I repeat, because I'm not entirely sure I heard her right.

Grant nods. 'Come here, give her a stroke.'

Amélie, it turns out, is an Angora rabbit. She has long, fluffy ears and an even fluffier body. Grant named her after the main character in one of her favourite films about someone who tries to do nice things for people.

'Did you know rabbits' teeth don't stop growing?' Grant says, and she seems completely different curled up on the floor with Amélie. It's like she's my age, and we're two friends chatting. 'So I need to make sure I give her tough food to eat.'

'Wow,' I say, reaching out for Amélie. At first, she seems nervous, but then Grant hands me a celery stick and I'm able to feed her with one hand and pet her with another. She decides, though, that she doesn't trust me quite yet because she snatches the second celery stick from me and runs off under a chair to eat it in peace.

'Did you know that the collective noun for rabbits is a colony?' I say to Grant. 'Same as ants.'

She smiles. 'I didn't know that! I always assumed they'd be called a burrow, or something, based on where they lived.'

I tell Grant that I like finding out the collective nouns for bugs, animals and birds.

'There are a few unexpected ones. Like a group of crows is called a murder, and a group of ravens is called a conspiracy. Birds have the most interesting collective nouns, in my opinion.'

'I agree,' Grant says, and I think she's happy that I'm starting to talk a bit more. Once my words start coming, they tumble out and I feel better having spoken them.

Once we've tidied up from breakfast, Grant shows me around.

'You can watch TV in the living room and feel free to borrow any books . . . If there's any food you would like in particular, let me know . . . I always do the shopping on a Thursday. Oh, and this room is locked because you're not allowed in there. No one is, besides me.'

She points to a door in the kitchen I almost hadn't noticed. It's next to the fridge and has the same wallpaper as the rest of the kitchen, so it blends in, almost as if it's supposed to be hidden. If she hadn't pointed it out

I would have walked right past it. Except, looking closer now, I can see there's a brass latch with a matching padlock hanging off it.

'Why?' I ask, a little curious. 'What's in there?'

'Just something private I'm working on,' says Grant, her voice a little higher-pitched than normal. 'We all like to keep some things to ourselves, don't we?'

I nod, understanding, because the fireflies are my secret. Right now I'm more interested in the garden, which, from the window, looks completely wild. Flowers grow as tall as me and there are windy paths through them. I bet there are loads of different bugs in there.

'I'll show you around the garden in a moment,' Grant says, following my eyeline. 'If you like.' But then, like the clouds hear us and want to ruin our day, it starts raining and I watch as Grant changes her morning schedule to 'work', instead of gardening. 'Don't worry, we'll have plenty of time. Why don't you unpack and get settled? You must be tired too, from the jetlag.'

I shrug. 'It's only a two hour difference, actually. But I'll probably be tired tonight.'

Later, in my room, as I'm unpacking, I notice the apple is gone from my bedside table. Eventually, I find it under my bed, nibbled at the edges, two rabbit-teeth markings giving it away.

I pick it up and inspect it. Apart from being quite large, it looks just like a normal apple. I stuff it in the drawer of my bedside table as a reminder – or a warning – of the fireflies, and their most recent visit.

CHAPTER 7

Being at school during the summer holidays should be banned. It's Monday, three days since I landed in England, and I'm waiting outside the classroom door of an empty, gloomy hallway at precisely 8.52 a.m.. I know this because the clock is tick, tick, ticking in the silence and I've been counting it ever since 8.27 a.m., when Grant had to drop me off.

Grant explained that she goes out for a few hours on Monday mornings, which means I need to be at school early. And since English is the only lesson I can take at this time, that's what I'm studying alongside my other subjects: art and practical biology. Even though I'm old enough, Grant and Mama and Dad decided I shouldn't be alone in a strange new house in a strange new country.

For some reason, no one thought to ask me my opinion.

'It'll help you settle in,' Grant explained that morning, echoing Mama's words. 'Get to know the curriculum. It'll be your school in September, after all.'

It was once Dad's school too, but I think it must be different now to how it was when he was here. It's very modern, with giant TV screens lining the hallways, and shiny floors. Everything is blue: the chairs, the floors, even the statue of a magpie at the centre of the main foyer.

'A charm,' I mutter to myself, reciting my favourite collective noun for that species of bird.

'Hello?' says a voice from down the hall. For a moment I think it's the fireflies, but then I notice a human-shaped silhouette in the distance.

'Hello?' I say, my voice echoing strangely along the barren halls.

'Hello,' says the voice again. I wonder if we'll just continue to say hello forever and ever, until the very same voice says something different as she approaches.

'I'm Ruby and I'm here for summer school,' she says confidently, holding out her hand. She's dressed very smartly, in a checked blazer and skirt. 'You are?'

'Hazel,' I say, less confidently. I'm wearing a pair of dark green dungarees and a lilac top that suddenly makes me feel underdressed.

'Are you sure about that?'

'Hmmm?' I say, a little confused.

'You just don't seem *sure* that's your name,' Ruby explains, a concerned frown on her face. Her hand is still hanging there, waiting for me to shake it, so I do.

'I . . . well . . . If I'm being honest, not really.' And that's when I tell her that I was named after the great-aunt I've only just met and that we seem nothing alike and that the name seems to fit her way more than it fits me. I also then explain that the reason I'm staying with my great-aunt is because my parents are moving us halfway across the world and so they've sent me here alone to 'settle in' while they sort everything out back home . . . Or not home, really, because *this* is now my home . . . And by the time I've stopped speaking I realise I've been talking non-stop for a few minutes and barely even taken a breath, my words tumbling over one another like excited puppies scrambling for food.

I expect Ruby to pull a face at me and turn away. People do that sometimes. Omar was used to it because we've known each other since we were babies, and anyway he would just tell me to shut up and get to the point. But that isn't what Ruby does. Instead, she says something really interesting.

'Names are important,' she begins. 'My mum says that the names we're assigned can shape who we are.'

That thought worries me, and so I chew it over before the worry grows too big. What future does a name like

Hazel hold? But I don't have much time to think about it because Ruby continues.

'My English name, for example,' she says, 'represents energy and success.'

'Wow,' I say. 'But you said "English name". Do you have a name in another language too?'

Ruby looks pleased by the question and nods. 'My middle name is from Japan, where my mum is from. It's Ai, and it means love and compassion. My parents thought very carefully about both names, and they thought they made a good balance.'

'I don't have a middle name,' I find myself saying, after I tell Ruby that I'm from two different countries too, and that we share one of them. Then I explain that I have my mama's last name, instead of my dad's, because he never really knew his parents and lived with his aunt, who I'm now living with.

Ruby looks interested in everything I'm saying and nods. 'I like that.'

The conversation suddenly halts and I feel a little nervous about the silence, so I decide to break it.

'So, yeah,' I say. 'Does having a middle name mean I don't have a future? Or maybe only half a future?'

Ruby thinks about this for a moment. Then shakes her head. 'I think it means that your future is a blank canvas for you to draw on.'

I almost laugh at this because it sounds like something a wise old person would say. Thinking about it, none of my life has been decided by me so far. And now I've been forced from one place to another without ever being asked what *I* want, I can't ever imagine deciding my own fate.

But before I can say any of that I hear the squeak of trainers as two boys walk up the hall together. They're both wearing similar clothes to one another – jeans and a hoodie – and suddenly I feel less casual. One of the boys has white skin and long light brown hair, the other has black skin and short black hair. They wave at us. Or, I realise, they must be waving at Ruby, because she nods back at them.

Suddenly, I feel very out of place, an outsider among friends. I miss Omar and how comfortable I felt around him. We talk as much as we can since he moved to America, mainly through our video games, but it isn't the same.

'We went to the same primary school,' Ruby explains, keeping me in the loop, like she can tell this is awkward for me. 'We're coming to this secondary school next year. Are you?'

I nod. Ruby seems pleased by this, which makes the knot in my stomach loosen a little.

Then I hear the jangling of keys and see a woman in a long floral dress and clear-framed glasses walk down the hall. She has brown skin and black hair that is tied up into a long ponytail. When she sees us, she smiles and unlocks the door into the dusty classroom. All the desks are empty, as if over the summer they're filled not with students, but ghosts.

CHAPTER 8

'And what about you, Hazel?' Ms Basra, our teacher, asks once everyone else has introduced themselves. The two boys, it turns out, are called Ezra and Akin, and they're at summer school because their parents work in the city and want them to have something useful to focus on. Ruby's parents work from home but *she* decided she wanted to do it. I'm not surprised after she told me her English name meant energy and success.

The community raised funds to put on the summer school so the village kids would have things to do. But most of them, it seems, have gone away on holiday to other exciting places. There's only us four from our year, and a few other groups in older years who Ms Basra looks after on different days.

We're the smallest class, apparently. I haven't been to my

other subject groups, but I know there's at least double in practical biology and even more in art. They're all people from different years, though, as 'the curriculum isn't as specific', according to the information on the website.

'Do you need a bit more time to think?' Ms Basra speaks again. I'm worried she's annoyed, but her face looks kind and sympathetic.

'Erm, well . . . I'm staying with my great-aunt for the summer before I start at this school in September. My parents are still in Kuwait, packing up our things, and so . . . that's why I'm here.'

Akin asks me questions about Kuwait, and he seems genuinely interested, but I don't really know what to say apart from it's hot and we have different weekend days, so our conversation ends quite quickly. 'My great-aunt has a house rabbit,' I add randomly, hoping it will break the awkward silence. It seems to be the right thing to say because suddenly everyone asks questions at once. Ezra's is 'Does it just poo on the floor in the house?'.

'I'm not sure, actually,' I say, worried I've ended the conversation again. But then Ruby speaks.

'Rabbits are considered good luck,' she explains, her voice rising above the others. 'And in Japanese folklore, rabbits live on the moon and make rice cakes there.'

'That's so cool!' I say, thinking Grant would like the second fact (I'm guessing she already knows the first).

Ruby doesn't really ask questions, I realise. She seems to answer them instead, even if you haven't asked. But that's OK, because I tell her my fact about a group of rabbits being called a colony, and then things are a little bit less scary.

Once we're done with that, Ms Basra explains that our theme for summer school this year is fairy tales.

'We're going to spend the first few weeks doing research. Now, who can tell me anything about fairy tales?' She stands, hands poised at the whiteboard, clearly hoping someone will offer an answer.

The window is open just a crack, enough to let in a cool breeze. It's raining again outside, and I can hear its pitter patter on the windowpane, the smell of wet grass, soaked to the roots, sneaking inside. I'm so used to dust and courtyards; this weather feels different, comforting somehow.

Ruby, of course, puts her hand up right away.

'You don't have to raise your hand, Ruby,' Ms Basra says with a smile. 'There's only five of us, so we can be a bit more informal.'

Ruby immediately drops her hand and starts speaking. 'A fairy tale is a story set in a faraway, make-believe land. It usually features a villain, and a main character who goes on some sort of quest. There is often a moral, and fairy tales teach us about things like our emotions –'

'Hang on,' Ms Basra interrupts, frantically writing what Ruby says in little phrases with clouds drawn around them on the board. 'All right, Ruby, stop right there. Thank you. Now for the first lesson let's focus on the setting. Make-believe, faraway lands . . .'

As Ms Basra speaks, I drink in the fresh air coming from the window, its wildness keeping me calm. But it brings something else with it, something treacherous that I hoped I could avoid, at least until this evening.

The fireflies.

The feeling of calm turns into a tightness in my chest as they land on my desk: all three of them.

I lean back abruptly, trying to get away from the fireflies, and my chair scrapes against the floor, making everyone glance over at me. Then, I sit on my hands, which are already scratched up from the fireflies' first visit. Maybe if they can't reach them this time, they'll leave me alone.

While Ruby and Ms Basra speak about fairy tales, and Akin and Ezra watch them, making notes, the fireflies place themselves on my shoulders, tugging at my top until I jerk my hand up to swat them away.

'Everything OK, Hazel?' Ms Basra asks, her voice gentle. It's hard to hide in a classroom of just four kids and one adult.

Ruby turns, a frown on her face. I think maybe she's annoyed I interrupted her, but she just looks worried.

'Oh, sorry,' I say. 'Can I, um, can I go to the toilet?'

Ms Basra smiles again, and I start to think 'happy' is her main mood. 'Of course, of course! Like I said, this isn't like normal school, so feel free to come and go, stand up and stretch your legs, things like that.'

Ezra immediately puts his hand up, even though he doesn't need to.

'Yes, Ezra?' Ms Basra says.

'Does that mean I can go home?'

Ms Basra lets out a snort laugh. 'Nice try,' she says. 'But no. Now, let's continue . . .'

While she carries on speaking, I quickly scuffle out of the classroom, the fireflies following me into the quiet hall.

The morning sun streams in through the windows as I slowly walk towards the bathroom. I dread to think what new quest is waiting for me around the corner.

There are mounted boards on the walls of the hall filled with pieces of work, proudly displayed. Poems about home, and love, and loss, with the occasional artwork to join it, drawn by some of the older students. There is one particular sketch that draws my attention. A mask, smiling, eyes creased in happiness. And then, next to it, the face it covers, empty sockets, tears spilling down. That's how I feel at the moment: like I'm having to hide my true feelings. Acting. Because no one seems to ever ask how I *really* feel about it all. Moving to England, living with Grant, making new friends.

The fireflies lead the way, pulling at my jeans, dragging me along. They're becoming more insistent now, more aggressive. Through some of the closed doors I can hear other groups of students chatting with teachers, some of them more rowdy than our class.

As I approach the end of the hall, with the toilets on the left, the white walls and grey marl floor begin to change. Gnarled roots line the walls; clumps of grass and wildflowers replace the skirting board. The closer I get to the toilets, the more everything transforms. Up ahead is a canopy of leaves and beyond it, birdsong.

I open the door to the toilets, but instead of a row of stalls and sinks, I'm met by a dense forest dotted with flowers.

The fireflies disappear into the gloom, their lights like pinpricks.

I peer ahead and step forward, my shoes sinking into the mossy path. I take one look behind me to see the entrance to the toilet has disappeared entirely. And, like I did on my first night in England, I follow them.

CHAPTER 9

As I step through what should have been the school toilets, the light disappears entirely, the canopy of leaves above blocking it out. The fireflies are my only way of seeing in the dark, and so I continue following them now, deeper into the forest than I've been before.

Everything is bigger here, scaled up: the trees, the fireflies, even my own shadow. Though I'm still the same size.

The bushes rustle as I walk, enclosing me on either side. I can hear snuffling, a distant howl, and closer, the heavy clop of hooves. It makes me jump, makes my heart pound in my chest like a caged bird desperate to get free. It's too dark for me to make out anything, so my brain fills in the gaps. Each shadow is a shape-shifting monster, threatening to swallow me whole.

I imagine giant claws reaching for my skin, and fangs

dripping with saliva.

Crunch.

Paws the size of my head that could crush my bones in seconds.

Crunch.

And wild animals surrounding me, the only sound their shallow breaths, hot on my face as they lean closer and closer and –

Crunch.

I jump, I turn, but there's nothing there. I turn back and the fireflies are gone. I'm alone. The air feels heavy here, weighing down on my chest, each breath I take a desperate gulp.

A single strand of light beams down ahead of me. I step into it, and that's when the whispers start, just as they have done each time before.

Do you have it? Do you have it? Do you have it?

'Have what?' I ask, though part of me knows what they're requesting.

The stolen fruit. The stolen fruit. The stolen fruit.

I fall silent, wondering how it is they know. I can smell danger in the air, like ash and smoke, and an instinct inside me is telling me they're angry, even though their voices are as enticing as they've always been.

'No,' I say, trying to sound confident, but it sounds more like a question.

Silence.

Then.

Lies. Lies. Lies.

My heart beats in time with the whispers.

And, like an orchestra of horrors, the voices continue.

Return the stolen fruit or pay the price. Return the stolen fruit or pay the price. Return the stolen fruit or pay the price.

I close my eyes and imagine what Ruby would say if she were in my position, and then I almost hear her voice coming out of my mouth: 'And what if I don't?'

The voices laugh. *Hiss, hiss, hiss.*

Try it, they say, three times, challenging me.

My mouth goes dry, my words beginning to shrivel up inside of me the way they did when I first landed in England. I try one more question before it's too late: 'What is the price I would pay?'

The price you pay is your deepest, darkest fears come true . . .

'I don't have any fears,' I declare, even though it's a lie. Because the fireflies' words remind me of something that happened shortly after the first time they visited. Mama and Dad had noticed the scratches on my hands, had listened to my stories about the firefly forest and the quest they sent me on – over and over – to pick piece after piece of fruit.

It was late, and so I should have been asleep instead of listening to them chat in the kitchen. I couldn't see them, through the door that was open just a crack, but I could hear them clearly.

'Is it our fault?' Dad had said to Mama, sniffing like he had a cold. 'Did we do something wrong?'

Mama usually has the answers to everything, so her next words had scared me.

'I don't know . . . Maybe?'

'We should have paid more attention when she first started telling us those stories,' Dad had said, sniffing again.

Mama sighed and I heard a patter of footsteps followed by the kettle turning on. 'What's important now is what we do next.'

I waited for Dad to respond and my heart sunk when he did. 'I'm just as bad as my parents. Maybe Hazel would be better off without us.'

'No, you're not,' Mama said, her voice fierce. 'You're nothing like your parents.'

Dad had started to cry then, properly cry, and I scrambled back to my room and pretended to be asleep when they checked on me ten minutes later.

Your parents will leave you here alone with Grant, just as your father's parents did to him, the fireflies say, interrupting my thoughts.

Hearing them voice my deepest, darkest fear, spell it out loud, makes my body turn cold and hot at once.

'H-how do you know that?' I ask, my voice barely a

whisper now.

But this time, they don't respond. The silence in here can be as scary as their words, because without instruction, I can't leave.

I've tried hard to ignore the fireflies before. I've tried to bat them away, but they stayed, scratching at my skin no matter where I went. I've tried to capture them too, but they freed themselves and punished me for it. And so I collected their fruit, obediently, for a moment of peace. But that peace never came – things only got worse.

But, a voice, my voice this time, reminds me. *Your parents got rid of the fireflies before.*

It's true, they did. But my parents aren't here now. And if I don't do the fireflies' quest, then they never will be.

What is your decision? What is your decision? What is your decision?

'I'll get the fruit,' I say with a shaking voice, determined that this will be my last task for them. 'When –?'

But the fireflies have gone.

A shroud of leaves rain down on me, stained a deep red. I watch as leaf after leaf falls listlessly to the floor, and I think of my hands, the way the fireflies pick, pick, pick at my skin, drawing blood.

An owl hoots, short and sharp. A door slams somewhere in the forest, causing birds to caw and scatter into the air. Light seeps in and I swear I see a silhouette ahead.

Is it a deer? Or a horse?

One blink and I'm back in the school toilets, just as Ruby walks through the door to fetch me.

'There you are!' she says, looking relieved. 'Where have you been?'

I don't respond, because I can't exactly tell her the truth, can I?

'Sorry,' I say instead.

Ruby rolls her eyes. 'Don't apologise. But come on, hurry,' she says excitedly. 'We're starting our first task, and Ms Basra brought SWEETS.'

I follow her out, like I followed my parents to the airport, Mo to the plane, Grant to her house, and the fireflies through the forest.

I wonder if I'll ever be the one leading the way.

CHAPTER 10

Over the next few days, Grant and I settle into a routine. Breakfast, lunch and dinner are always at the same time, though the day-to-day activities change. Sometimes Grant works at her desk in the little library section of her living room, other times she renovates various parts of her old house. One afternoon we had no electricity because Grant was rewiring it, and another we had no water because she was sorting out the plumbing. Grant seems to be able to do everything herself, without the help of anyone else. I can't imagine *ever* being that way.

Sometimes I hear her checking her little room in the kitchen when I'm not in there, and the more she does the more curious I am to know what's inside it. The click of the padlock and creak of the door is familiar to me now.

The days go by quickly between summer school, helping Grant round the house and catching up with Omar online. We play games on our computers and he shows me all the videos he took of his trip to Disneyland. In Art on Wednesday we had to do still life, which means we select an object to draw. I chose the apple I picked from the forest, which I keep with me at all times, in case the fireflies call. It was interesting because apples aren't round and red like our brains make us believe. They have bumps and bruises like humans, and shades that blend into different colours. I ended up using blues and purples and yellows and oranges too, for the bit Amélie nibbled.

I can't help but think of the fireflies' threat about the price I'll pay unless I return the apple. I try to keep my deepest, darkest fears just out of sight in my mind, like the creatures in the forest lurking in the shadows. But what if both come out to hunt me?

Now it's the weekend and today is the first full day since I arrived that it hasn't rained, so Grant finally shows me properly around her garden. It starts at the side of the house, by the kitchen door. There are mismatched paving slabs that wind like a breadcrumb trail up to a hedged arch. Beyond, I glimpse more paving stones, surrounded by flowers. They wind in several different paths around the garden; in and among them are little signs with words like 'Rose Cove' and 'Geranium Avenue'.

'These are one of my favourites,' Grant says, showing me a group of flowers that droop downwards, so they look like tiny purple bells. 'They're called foxgloves, but people know them as fairy bells because it's believed that fairies live in them . . . But look, there actually *is* something living in this one. Can you see?'

Grant's whispering now, moving slowly, clasping the stem of the flower gently. I look inside, half expecting to find a fairy, like she said, but instead I'm met with something that looks a bit like a green bean.

'What is it?' I ask.

'A caterpillar's cocoon!' says Grant, in a loud whisper. 'Soon it'll be a butterfly. I found it the other day, before you'd arrived and . . . Well, I thought you'd be interested to watch its journey.'

Now that I know what it is, I imagine the little caterpillar shifting in form inside the bean-like thing. In Practical Biology, yesterday, we were given mystery seeds to grow and tend over the summer. I'm still not sure what mine are, but the winner gets a tree sapling of their own to plant at home. I think Grant might like it if I win.

'Did you know there are lots of different names for a group of butterflies,' I say. 'My least favourite are swarm and rabble because that makes it seem as if you don't want them there. My favourite is flutter, and kaleidoscope.'

'Oh,' says Grant. 'I like kaleidoscopes because their

patterns sort of look like the scales on butterfly wings, don't you think?'

I agree, and we decide to give the caterpillar peace to grow and change as we move on to other sections of the garden.

Grant's garden seems endless, like a world of its own. The further in we go, the more I feel like it's hugging me in a warm embrace full of beautiful scents and the lazy haze of summer. It's completely alive too, with thousands of little creatures roaming around. There are spiders and woodlice and ants and beetles. I can hardly keep up with them all. But they keep up with us, the soft buzzing of a whole world of bugs follows us around as we inspect.

Grant tells me the names of lots of different flowers, and even shows me some edible ones. I almost gasp when I see her put one in her mouth and chew it, and try it myself. At first, it kind of feels like I'm eating a butterfly, the petals tickling the inside of my cheeks. But as I chew there's a slight bitter taste, and it's more like I'm having a salad.

When we finally reach the end of Grant's garden, her house is the size of an apple behind us. Her garden is like its very own world. I realise the sound of running water I heard on my first night in England was coming from here, because surrounding the garden's edge is a stream that winds in and around the flowers, flowing into a pond.

It's filled with lily pads and other plants poking out of the water and . . .

'A frog!' I can't help but squeal out loud.

Grant laughs. 'There are a lot of those around. Do you know what a group of frogs is called?' she asks, raising an eyebrow.

I realise, I don't.

'An army.' Grant seems pleased to be able to share this with me, and I repeat it three times, so I can remember it.

Later, I'm supposed to be researching fairy-tale settings for my homework, but instead I keep looking up all of the bugs I found in Grant's garden. I'm in Dad's room – my room – and it's still weird being in here, but it feels comforting too. It has imprints of him left behind. Posters of his favourite musicians, faded wallpaper covered in photos of him with friends at school, ties wrapped around their heads to celebrate them moving on to adulthood.

In the pictures my dad still has the same smile, the same carefree attitude seeping from him that I could never muster myself. Mama has the same ability. Moving seems easy for them both. They can bend to whatever comes their way, like wheat stalks in the wind.

I'm like a tree, rooted to the spot, unsure of how I can fare in different conditions. And after spending a little time with Grant in her home, I wonder if she's the same too.

Then there are tickets to concerts and festivals, and eventually plane-ticket stubs to trail Dad's journey across the world. A worn map, its edges curling, hangs at the back of the bed, colourful pins to mark the countries he planned to visit.

I scan the pins for the one that marks my home, where my parents had met. It was a bit of a fairy tale: they both attended a mutual friend's party and 'hit it off' as they liked to say. They spoke until the sun rose and decided to go for breakfast. Then, after two years they married. And that was it.

Dad's room stops telling the story of his life after that: after he moved to Kuwait and met Mama and had me. I wish the wall could tell me the future as well as the past, so I can find out if my fears of Mama and Dad leaving me here alone with Grant will come true.

After a while I realise I've got even more distracted from my work. I unplug the laptop from the little desk and crawl into bed instead with the laptop over the duvet.

Somehow, my fairy-tale homework research leads me down a bit of a rabbit hole, and I end up stumbling across the real story of Rapunzel. It starts off with her parents stealing fruit from a witch's garden. It makes me think of the half-eaten apple I've been carrying around, now starting to rot. So then I look up fireflies and fruit and discover something a little weird: fireflies *eat* each other. I wonder if maybe there were once many more of them, and now there are only three. The fact that they are cannibals makes me shiver.

But I sort of hope the last three eat each other, so they don't bother me, and that's when an email pings up on my laptop, from a school email address.

Hello!!

I wasn't sure if you've had the chance to do your homework yet, so I thought I'd show you what I found. There's an article about loads of cool haunted forests around the world. They're all cursed and lead people to their deaths. There are ghosts and goblins and scary spirits. Seems fun, right? Oh, and one even has these dolls hanging all over the trees. When you look closely at the dolls you can see them move their arms or heads. By the way, I've chosen the Black Forest, so as long as you don't go for that one, you can pick any of the others. I looked up creepy forests because Ms Basra said a lot of fairy-tale settings are scary at first. She used the example of Snow White. You know the film? Where she's in the forest and all these eyes stare at her? If you search 'Snow White and the Haunted Forest' you'll find the clip she played for us while you were in the bathroom.

Also, I looked up the meaning of your name for you and did you know that it's both an Arabic and English name? So even though you're named after your great-aunt, it's kind of yours too. I'm sure you already know Hazel's a kind of tree, but I don't know if you're aware that hazelnuts were used in lots of medicines and the tree is a symbol of peace and health, which my mum says is very auspicious (that means promising or favourable).

Anyway, I need to go practise my clarinet. See you Monday. :)

Ruby

I reply to thank Ruby for the homework help and for looking up my name, and I ask her what a clarinet is, because I've never heard of it. Then I search for the video she mentions. It opens with someone telling Snow White to run away into the woods. She looks afraid, but goes anyway. The woods are dark, vines clinging on to her as she runs through, unable to see. A pair of eyes peer at her from one of the trees and it turns out to be an owl. Then some bats.

The trees seem to reach for her, grabbing her dress, and it reminds me a little too much of *my* forest and the trees I've grown familiar with. Everything in the forest twists into something more sinister, and Snow White gets so scared she collapses.

When I look further into Snow White, I find out later she eats a poisoned apple that puts her into a cursed sleep. I think of the bite Amélie took from my apple and finish looking up Rapunzel. It turns out that she's taken by a witch because her mother ate the stolen fruit while she was pregnant.

Fairy tales and fruit, it seems, are closely linked.

Sneaking downstairs, I find Amélie asleep in her usual spot in front of the secret door in Grant's kitchen. It's like she's guarding it. I bend down to stroke her – she seems used to me now – and she doesn't *seem* like she's been poisoned. But then again, I don't know how I'd tell until it was too late. At least, though, she's not been stolen by a witch.

Thanks to Ruby, I finish my homework fairly quickly, but I can't get the apple out of my head. If I return it, will the fireflies mind that it's had a piece bitten off it? Will they know it was Amélie and not me?

Whenever I looked up fruit in fairy tales the same word kept cropping up: curse. It floats around in my mind, but I bat it away like a fly.

This is silly. I'm being silly. I'm seeing connections in things that don't exist and letting my imagination run wild.

Still, I can't help but wonder: what'll happen when the fireflies come next?

CHAPTER 11

'Hazel? Hazel!' Ms Basra says and I snap out of my daydream. I had been worrying about returning to the firefly forest ever since I discovered the thing about the poisoned apple. The apple I had stolen from the fireflies is in my bag. The skin is turning dark and soft. The smell it leaves behind is sickly sweet, and having it here feels as if I'm closing the gap between my world and the firefly forest.

'Sorry, Ms,' I say. The truth is, I haven't slept well over the last few days. I find myself crawling in and out of bed at night to make sure Amélie is OK. I keep imagining the fireflies have taken her to their forest as punishment, the way Rapunzel was snatched by the witch; or else, I imagine her poisoned, like Snow White, her lifeless body cold on the kitchen floor.

Grant found me one night checking on her and I tried

to pretend I was sleepwalking, but it didn't work. She told me off and said it was 'way too late for someone of your age to be up'. It was only just gone midnight.

That's another difference between England and Kuwait: there everyone stays up late because of the heat. Here they go to bed early and wake with the sun.

'Can you tell us a bit about the forest you researched?' Ms Basra continues with a smile.

'Yes!' I say and turn to my page of notes. Once I'd dragged myself away from the whole Snow White thing, the research was interesting.

'All right,' Ms Basra says in a sing-song voice. 'Start by telling us the name of the forest, introduce it to us and let us know your three facts. Ezra, Akin and Ruby, you're to do the same when it's your turn.'

I stand up for some reason, because it feels the right thing to do while I'm presenting.

'The forest I have chosen to research is Highgate Cemetery in London.' I peer around the room, making sure not to look directly at any of the others. I have a slight American accent that I picked up from school back home. Even though I've been trying to sound more like Ruby and the others – soften my 'r's and squish up my syllables – it's still different to everyone else. 'I find it interesting because you wouldn't expect to find a forest in the middle of a city. My three facts are: It is where Bram Stoker set Dracula, which is all about vampires. The cemetery was established in the 1800s, and lots of people claim they have seen a vampire leaning over the graves.'

Only when I finish do I look at Ruby. She grins at me, and it feels like a dolphin is swooping in my chest, showing off. I sit back down and try to relax now that my part is over.

'Well done, Hazel!' says Ms Basra, seemingly pleased. 'What a great example. And yes, you're right, the supernatural and spooky can be found where we least expect them. A forest doesn't need to be out in the middle of nowhere. It could be right next door in a well-known city.'

Or even inside the school bathrooms, I think, but I just nod at Ms Basra instead.

'And it's interesting,' continues Ms Basra, 'that you mention Dracula because Bram Stoker based the book on a well-known legend, and as we know that is the source of many fairy tales. Dracula also uses other fairy-tale tropes, such as castles and, of course, forests. So, well done, Hazel for such a thoughtful example. Now who's next?'

'Mine's really boring in comparison,' Akin says.

'I'm sure it's not, Akin,' replies Ms Basra encouragingly. He ends up telling us all about Sherwood Forest where Robin Hood was from. Then Ezra talks about the forest they filmed *Lord of the Rings* in, which Ms Basra tries really hard to connect to fairy tales, but can't, until she mentions the book and its inspirations.

It's Ruby's turn. She stands up, like I did, her black hair shining in the artificial light, hanging down her back, swishing as she speaks. Ruby talks about the Black Forest in Germany, as she had mentioned she would in her email. She explains that it was the setting of many of the Brothers Grimm fairy tales. She mentions stories of lurking wolves, and a headless horseman with an underwater lair. It sounds really creepy, especially when Ruby says that the forest is filled with fir trees, which let hardly any sunlight filter through it.

I think of the firefly forest again, and how I need the fireflies to help me navigate it. Shadows follow me around, leaves rustle and crunch. Were those shadows wolves? Or the headless horseman?

The price you pay is your deepest, darkest fears come true. That's what the fireflies said. But my fears are quickly growing: I'm afraid I've hurt Amélie; I'm afraid my parents are going to leave me here alone with Grant. And I'm afraid that, one day, the fireflies will trap me in the forest for good.

CHAPTER 12

It's a short walk home from school, which Grant lets me do on my own now that I'm getting familiar with the area. Near the school, at the centre of the village, there's a little square of shops: a post office, café, fish and chip place and doctor's surgery, as well as a bus stop to the nearest city. There are modern houses lined up neatly in rows, but closer to Grant's house it's just fields filled with cows munching on grass, the houses spread out like pollinating bumblebees.

Back home in Kuwait, I'd got used to sitting in a stuffy car every afternoon, when the sun was high, the seat burning my legs in the heat. But here the sun is different. It hangs lower and the sunsets go on for much longer. Instead of dipping down suddenly, they paint the sky pink and purple. That's the next thing I want to draw in art class.

I guess everyone living in England must be used to it, because I never notice anyone else really looking at the sky, but every day it has a new story to tell, and looking upwards is the one way I can feel calm about all of the changes happening in my life.

Grant's home is down a windy path with ditches on either side of it filled with streaming water that I think connects to the stream in her garden. Overgrown grass and wheat stalks blow in the wind. It's raining a little, leaving a sheen on the brick buildings and concrete road ahead. There are no pavements down the lane, and occasionally a car has to slow down as it approaches, squeezing past me, while my socks get wet on the muddied grass.

The drizzle is slowly frizzing up my hair. I pass by several of Grant's neighbours, all cosy inside their homes, and remind myself that I'll be the same in a few minutes. One of them has a Shetland pony that lives in a medium-sized paddock. It's white and brown and seems to be enjoying the rain as it trots around. Grant's gingerbread house is just a little further on, at the very end of the lane. The building is made of a light stone, with cornices around the windows that resemble white icing. There's a small white fence at the front, straight out of a storybook, a stony path leading to a heavy wooden door, and the garden to the side.

As it happens, I don't get a chance to escape the rain like Grant's neighbours, because the Shetland pony approaches me, and that's when I see them. The three fireflies sit atop its head as it trots over to me. It's as if they're controlling its movements.

The pony bows its head and the fireflies fly, one at a time, swirling around my head, twirling towards a bush just beyond the paddock.

This is the moment I've been waiting for. The apple is tucked in my backpack, along with a small head torch I found in Grant's kitchen. Better to see the forest with.

I follow the fireflies into the hedgerow and get stung by a bunch of nettles, which I only just learned about for the first time in Practical Biology. I feel a sharp pain up my left ankle and wish I had a dock leaf to soothe it, but I haven't got time to stop and find one. As I crawl through the brambles I close my eyes, little twigs scratching my cheeks. It reminds me of the video Ruby sent me of Snow White, though I try to ignore the thought. On the other side, where the top of the paddock should have stood, is the mouth of the firefly forest open wide. Waiting.

It's time for me to complete my next quest: return the stolen apple and stop my deepest, darkest fears from coming true.

I reach into my backpack and put on the head torch just as the fireflies disappear, zigzagging between the trees. I follow, less afraid now that I can see ahead of me, even if it is only a metre or so in front. But still the rustles, still the howls; they seep down my throat and into my chest, making my breath catch like a trapped birds' wings. Eventually, accompanying them, are the whispers.

Do you have it? Do you have it? Do you have it?

'Yes,' I say, my voice ringing loud and clear this time. 'I do.'

A *crunch* to my right. I whip my head round and see something disappear behind a tree. I'm sure it's the same creature whose shadow I had spotted before. This time, I'm determined to catch it. After all, shadows and monsters aren't scary so long as you know what they are. Right?

Show us. Show us. Show us.

I pull out the apple, now soft, juice sliding down my wrist from the yellowing bite of Amélie's teeth.

The fireflies fly to my outstretched palm to pluck the apple from it. I feel them scratch, scratch, scratch, as they do and it sends shivers down my spine.

Silence.

Then: *This won't do. This won't do. This won't do.*

My heart sinks. Part of me knew they'd say this, but the other part had hoped they would let it pass.

Crunch. From just behind me. I whip round to see a swishing white tail disappear in the gloom. I can hear the rhythmic clopping of horse's hooves before the whispers take over once more.

'Why?' I ask in frustration, thinking back to my deepest,

darkest fears in my world and theirs.

You must complete a forfeit. You must complete a forfeit. You must complete a forfeit, the fireflies reply.

'What forfeit?' I ask.

Bring us the key. Bring us the key. Bring us the key.

'What key?' I ask through gritted teeth, my frustration growing.

Crunch. To my left, this time. I turn and see the side of a horse, a shining brown boot kicking at it, attached to a leg.

'Please, I wish you would *help* me,' I say desperately. 'What key do you need?'

Knock on wood. Knock on wood. Knock on wood.

'Why?' I ask, confused. I'm getting frustrated now by their requests.

You must knock on wood or the tree spirits will make sure your wish doesn't come true.

'I didn't make a wish,' I snap, frustration mingling with fear.

Yes you did. Yes you did. Yes you did, they hiss. And I realise I'd wished for their help.

Knock on wood. Knock on wood. Knock on wood, the voices echo. *Or the spirits won't let us tell you.*

I turn to the tree on my left. I knock on it three times, for each utterance of the instruction, and wait to find out where to get the key.

A hiss, like a rattle all up and down the trunk. I place

my hands on the tree and feel it rumble and shake.

Well done. Well done. Well done. The spirits will leave you be.

I let out a relieved sigh, waiting now for the fireflies to tell me where to find the key, and for the firefly forest to spit me back out. But they don't, and it doesn't.

What are you waiting for? the voices echo again.

'What do you mean?' I roar, confused. They're tricking me, somehow, but I don't understand their games.

You must knock on every tree. Every tree. Every tree.

I gulp the air and stare at the forest surrounding me on all sides.

'*Every* tree?'

Yes. Yes. Yes, the voices whisper. *You'd better hurry. Hurry. Hurry. Or else you can't complete your quest and you'll be trapped here forever. Forever. Forever.*

I freeze for a moment as the first of my deepest fears echo back to me. I need to find out where to get the key and get out of here, and hope (though I don't dare wish) that it's finally the end of their requests.

I run through the forest, knocking on each tree three times, until a stitch builds in my chest and my knuckles become red and raw. I swap hands, but both turn red by the time I reach the final tree, what seems like hours later.

And behind me, always behind me, the crunch of hooves on fallen leaves and twigs.

When I finally knock on the last tree, its rattle

reverberates around me adding to all the rest, so loud my insides beg for peace. Then I see it.

The horse, and the person atop it, bathed in the light from my torch.

Except, I can't quite tell if it's a person.

There is a pair of feet, attached to a pair of legs, attached to a body, which is holding an axe.

But where a head should be there is nothing.

The headless body jumps down from the horse and lifts an axe over its shoulders as it approaches. I hear the sound of blade against wind, and a *crunch*. I hear a scream, thinking for a moment that it's my own, until I look up and see it. One of the trees has blocked the creature with its branches, and its axe is stuck in it, as it rains down blood-like sap on me.

In that moment I know that some monsters are better left to the shadows. I turn and run, the tree's screams and the wind howling against the creature's hollow neck following me down the lane.

And, beneath all of that, the whispers:

The horseman has the key. The horseman has the key. The horseman has the key.

CHAPTER 13

'Where have you been?' shouts Grant. I've just slipped the house key into the door when she yanks it open, dragging me forward with it.

I'm not really sure what to say. The clock on the mantelpiece in the kitchen reads half six. It's a few hours past the end of summer school, and half an hour past dinnertime. I expect to see plates or food on the table, because Grant is never late for dinner (or any of her scheduled activities), but there aren't.

Grant looks me up and down, at my leaf-covered body, at the mud on my jeans, and my red-raw knuckles. Her face is pulling lots of different expressions and it seems as if she's trying to decide whether to settle on concerned or angry.

'I . . .' I say again, my lips shaking, tears building up. 'I . . .'

Grant looks worried now. 'What happened?'

'I . . .' I say for the third time. 'Fell.'

'Where?' Grant asks immediately, sounding a bit sceptical. 'I walked to school and back and I didn't see you anywhere!' Her voice rises and falls like a piece of music, ending on a high, shrill note.

'Into a ditch,' I say. 'Well, not really. I sort of half slipped in. Erm, I was walking home from school, and I fell. I mean slipped.'

Grant pauses. 'Are you sure that's what happened?' she asks, her eyes searching for the truth. 'I was just about to call your parents, I . . . Well . . .' She sits down on the stool, looking dazed. 'Your father never . . . I'm too old for this.'

'I'm sorry, Grant,' I say. 'I was with my friend Ruby.' Grant's eyes light up at the word 'friend', which spurs me on, 'and I . . . went round to her house for a bit after school as she plays the clar-clar-clari –'

'Clarinet?' Grant offers.

'Yes! And, well, I wanted to check it out so . . . Well, so when you went looking for me I wouldn't have been walking home, I would have been at hers. And then, when I *did* walk home I fell . . . I mean, slipped,' I finish flatly, my cheeks flushing at the lie I have just told.

Grant stares at me for a moment in total silence. Then she sighs.

'While I'm glad you're making friends and settling in

well here, you can't just run off whenever you like. I don't know what it was like in your parents' household but here I have rules. I'm going to have to tell them about this . . .'

'N-no!' I say. 'Please don't! I won't do it again, I promise.'

If Grant tells my parents about me disappearing, they'll know the fireflies are back. And then the worst of my deepest fears will come true: they'll leave me here alone with Grant, like Dad's parents left him. Dad will think he's been a bad parent and decide the job isn't for him. And Mama will follow, because they're a team.

No. I won't let that happen. I need to be like Grant, sorting everything out on my own. So that's what I'm going to do: retrieve the key from the horseman and everything will be OK and normal again.

Grant chews her lip, and glances at the clock anxiously. 'I suppose it's a little late there now . . .' She looks lost, pacing back and forth, and I feel guilty for the stress I put her under, even though it wasn't my fault. And I feel even guiltier for lying, but the fireflies haven't given me a choice.

'Shall we have some food?' I offer.

'Hmmm?' Grant says, her eyes are empty now. 'Oh no, it's too late for that.'

I glance at the clock. It's only seven. I used to eat much later with my parents.

'Oh,' I say, a little confused.

After a moment Grant gets up quietly and returns to her

desk in the living-room library. I peer at her schedule on the fridge and notice that 7–9 p.m. is dedicated to reading.

I decide to get myself a big bowl of cereal and eat it alone at the kitchen table. Amélie hops in some time later and I watch her scour the kitchen for food that might have been dropped on the floor. Her whiskers twitch with her little nose. She slowly makes her way towards me and looks up at me with her blood-red eyes.

'Fine,' I say, and I go into her snack tin and get her a few treats. She's probably worried about Grant too. The guilt of it all stabs me in the gut. My parents, when I've upset them, tell me off. But Grant just shrivelled up like a snail hiding inside its shell.

As Amélie bounds away, I notice the usually padlocked door is open. The one I'm not allowed to enter. My fingers tingle the way they do when the fireflies are calling me. What could be such a big secret that Grant keeps it locked in a strange room?

I tiptoe across the tiled floor, my socks not making a sound, and pull the door open. It's dark, and it's hard to see anything inside. I notice a light switch attached to a string on the ceiling, with a wooden handle at the bottom of it carved into the shape of a rabbit. I pull it and the lights turn on.

On rows and rows of shelves are jars filled with confusing shapes that twist and float in a sickly neon-yellow-green liquid. I don't have much time to take them in or understand what I'm seeing because I hear a scream from behind me.

I turn to see Grant watching me, wild-eyed. I leap out of the storeroom as she rushes to the door, switches the light off and slams it shut.

When she looks at me now her eyes are alive, crazed.

'Go to your room!' she shrieks, her face flushed. 'I told you never to go in there. You can't, you . . . Go to your room!'

I'm frozen to the spot, though my face is heating up. It's like Grant is a completely different person. Neither of us move for a moment. Then I step back and turn, running up to my room and slamming the door. I hide beneath the covers, every sound from below sending a zap of fear through my body, until I fall asleep.

CHAPTER 14

Over the next few days I make sure to follow Grant's timetable. We tiptoe around each other in a strange dance, barely speaking. Grant spends most of her days in the garden, while I wander around the house. If the thing with the secret door hadn't happened, I imagine I'd be outside with her. But now I've seen the door, and her reaction to me looking inside the room, it's as if I'm meeting a whole new Grant. I have so much I want to ask, but whenever I look in her direction, she glances away, like she's carrying a secret in her eyes.

On the days I'm not at summer school, usually I'd play games on my computer with Omar, but he's camping this week so this makes me feel even more alone.

Recently I found a crack in the wall of one corner of the kitchen, where a colony of ants crawl through. I count them like I used to at home and it makes me feel safe, even though everything is different. I keep glancing back at the locked door, trying to make sense of what I'd seen but I can't. And I know I won't unless I investigate further.

I've tried the combination to the padlock a few times, but nothing's worked so far. Four numbers. I tried 0000, 1234, and random years that might be special to Grant. When that didn't unlock it I looked up how long it would take to get the code right if I went up in sequence. 112 hours, which is over four days of constant guessing. I don't have that much time, especially as I'm sneaking around.

I just need to find the right moment, when Grant's not around, to get in another way . . . Usually I'd be worried about getting caught, but she's already mad at me, so how much worse can it get?

I look up and recite some new collective nouns, whenever I'm feeling worried or scared. My favourites that I've learned so far are: a cauldron of bats, a caravan of camels, and a prickle of porcupines.

Mama and Dad had promised to call weekly, but they miss our second call because they're 'busy tying up affairs', according to the email Dad sent. For some reason, I imagine them tying up fairies in their living room, maybe the ones that live in Grant's foxgloves. It makes me wonder if my two worlds are colliding and if the fireflies are somehow stopping my parents from contacting me to make my deepest, darkest fear come true. Will I only get to speak to Mama and Dad once I collect the key from the horseman?

When Dad asks how things are going with Grant in his email, I want so much to ask him about the room with the jars, but I don't think he'd understand. Plus, I'm worried that if I say anything, she'll mention that I came home late and they'll somehow find out that the fireflies are back, as I don't think I could lie to them like I could to Grant. So instead I tell them about school and fairy tales and make sure absolutely never to mention the fireflies.

They said they were proud of how well I was dealing with everything, and so I can't let them know the truth.

'Hazel!' Grant calls me down at just around 5 p.m. It's too early for dinner, so I worry something is wrong. Has she found out I tried the padlock?

I make my way downstairs to see Grant boiling something in a great big pot on the stove; she's stirring it like a witch stirs her cauldron, throwing in herbs like they're ingredients in a potion.

'Can you make some dumplings for dinner?' she says, without turning around. It's as if she has eyes in the back of her head. I try to peer closer at her hair to see if I can find a glimpse of lashes or pupils, but I can't. 'We're having stew and dumplings.'

She nods to the counter next to her, where a bunch of ingredients are laid out in front of an open book. It's an ancient book that looks like it was written a hundred years ago, and I half expect it to contain a spell, but it's just instructions for making dumplings.

As I mix the ingredients together, and watch the dough gain consistency, I find it relaxing to shape the mixture into balls, like playing with clay.

When it's time to eat, I take a tentative bite of the dumpling, followed by a spoonful of stew.

'It's delicious!' I say, forgetting for a moment that things are awkward between us.

'Thank you, Hazel,' Grant says, with a smile. But it's different, less friendly than it was. And she doesn't say anything more the way she usually would.

As Grant eats, I think about the fireflies and the key they want me to collect. The next time they come for me I'll have to face the headless horseman before I'm allowed back home again. The dread of it all comes back, like a wave washing over me.

That's when I feel it. The tingling sensation in my hands. I cover them up out of habit, embarrassed by how badly they're scratched at the moment, especially after knocking on trees.

The fireflies float into the room, hovering above Grant and me. I do my best not to look up at them so she doesn't notice and ask questions.

Amélie either senses my tension or can feel their

presence, because she leaps from the chair (where she usually sits between us for scraps of food) and darts out into the hall.

'What's wrong, Amélie?' says Grant, getting up to follow, just as the fireflies land one by one by one on my knuckles. I grip my knife and fork firmly, trying to ignore them, but they begin scratch, scratch, scratching.

I stand up, scrape my chair back, and make my way towards the hall. If the fireflies are going to force me away now I need to be somewhere private, where Grant can't see.

'What's going on?' Grant says, re-entering the room with a frenzied Amélie in her arms. She's scratching at Grant, desperate to get away, and Grant puts her down, torn between the two of us, until her eyes rest on me. I can't tell whether she is angry or concerned, her facial expressions for both emotions are the same. Her skin, accented by the T-shaped frown on her forehead, reminds me of the dough I had just mixed; part of me wants to smooth out Grant's expression, so I don't have to explain my odd behaviour.

'I –' I say, gripping my hands together, picking at my skin. 'I'm not feeling very well.'

My stomach rumbles and it sounds like a frog is trapped inside it. I fidget with the sleeves of my top, hiding my hands from the fireflies even though I know it won't work. They crawl up my arms scratch, scratch, scratching at my elbow, and I let out an involuntary twitch, my eyes now streaming with frustrated tears.

I start to feel hot, to feel panicked, and Grant steps closer, making everything worse. 'Well, of course you don't, you've barely eaten.' She hovers over me now and checks my forehead. I feel clammy, like I'm about to pass out, but Grant's touch is like magic, sending a zap, like an electric shock through me. 'Oh!' Grant giggles, a proper smile this time. 'Static.'

Her hands are surprisingly cold, soothing. They feel strong, the skin calloused, like armour against the fireflies.

The shock of Grant's touch sends the fireflies straight out of my sleeve and down the hall. They've never disappeared before. But why? Are they afraid of Grant?

'I feel better now,' I say shakily, sitting back down to finish my meal. I know Grant won't stop fussing until I do. 'I was just a little light-headed, that's all.'

The frog in my stomach grumbles again.

Amélie crawls back into the room and settles by my feet, shaking like a leaf in the winter breeze. When I finish my dinner, I pick her up and place her on my lap, stroking her gently. Eventually, after a few moments, she falls asleep.

CHAPTER 15

I peer at the jasmine which lines one entire side of Grant's house – a blend of green and white. The flowers are shaped like stars, waiting to be picked. There are two windows on this side of the house: one leads to Grant's secret storeroom, and the other to her bedroom. But because the house is so higgledy-piggledy, the window to the storeroom is too high up for me to reach, even with my arms stretched tall.

It's the middle of the night, and all the lights are off. It's taken a while to pluck up the courage to explore Grant's storeroom again, besides trying the padlock a few times. I need to understand what's in there, to know who I'm dealing with. If the fireflies are afraid of her, I want to know why. It might help me figure out how to scare them away. It's all I can do besides telling her the truth, and risking my parents leaving me forever.

I manage to sneak out the kitchen door and into the garden with only the moon and stars for company to try and climb in through the window instead. The fragrance of the jasmine guides me, sending me into a dreamlike trance. That's kind of what it feels like to move abroad. One moment you are grounded, and everything is familiar. You drink in the changes, sip them like an overly sweet hot chocolate. And then the next, you've had too much and it's like it's weighing you down, making you feel sick.

It's cold for a summer evening, the wind whipping round my dressing gown, sneaking in where I haven't wrapped it tight enough. It's like a spirit searching for a new body to possess. There's rain pat, pat, pattering on the ground, while the wind howls. I swear I can hear it whisper things to me, and I turn a couple of times in fear of seeing the fireflies.

They haven't returned since Grant chased them away, and even though that's meant to be a good thing I'm worried they'll make my deepest, darkest fears come true unless I retrieve the key from the horseman.

The ladder sits at the base of the jasmine wall, tucked in among the gravel. I carefully pick it up and place it against the wall, to the right of the storeroom window. I push down on the ladder to make sure it's steady. It reverberates in my hands and groans beneath my weight. I wish there was someone here to hold the bottom of the ladder, catch me when I fall, but there isn't. And then I remind myself I'm trying to be independent, like Grant. I have to risk it, like some lone traveller in search of treasure.

But when I think about what's really in that room, it doesn't seem like treasure at all.

I climb up to the fourth rung of the ladder and turn my head torch on low to peer in. The one I used in the firefly forest. I found it in one of Grant's drawers, which has old tins filled with needles and thread, plasters and matchboxes, and random wires. It was funny because all of Grant's house is so neat and orderly, from the kitchen cupboards through to the tables and cushions. Apart from that drawer. It's like a glimpse into her mind beyond the rules. The bit she keeps hidden from me, like the items locked in her storeroom.

The torch is too bright and turns the window into a mirror. Reflected in front of me, instead of the jars, is my own face, like a ghost staring back at me, hollow-eyed.

I try to open the window instead; it budges a little but is stuck fast. It's one of those windows that hangs on old pieces of string that you need to pull up instead of out. I put all my weight into it, and my foot slips off the ladder, making it wobble dangerously. I look down and I know it's not that far to fall, but the ground is gravelly and it would hurt.

I feel hot in my dressing gown now, sweating, but I climb on to the window ledge to get into a better position. It's old and made of wood, painted in a white gloss, like icing. It wobbles even more than the ladder did, but this way I can pull up, rather than push.

I try once more and the window opens with ease, raining dirt on my shoes. I go to step back on to the ladder and reposition myself to peer in, but I accidentally kick it, knocking it to the floor beneath the window.

CRASH.

The sound of metal on stone. So loud it's like an explosion.

A creak from Grant's bed, and further creaks beyond as she rushes down the stairs.

My heart leaps in my chest.

If I stay on the window ledge, Grant will see me, but she'll notice if I jump off too. So I do the only thing I can. I climb into the storeroom, shut the window behind me as quietly as I can, and switch the torch off.

I can hear Grant's slippers against the gravel coming closer. Then, I hear her pick up the ladder and set it up against the wall with a scrape. Soon after she's back in the kitchen, and I can hear her mumble beneath the crack of the door. She's speaking to Amélie: 'Don't worry, my sweet. It was just the wind.'

I count to one hundred in the dark, after I hear Grant's

bedroom floor squeak, just to make sure she's asleep. And then I switch the torch on, wishing almost at once that I hadn't.

It's hard to describe what's in Grant's storeroom, but I know now why she doesn't want me to see it. There are shelves from the floor to the ceiling filled with different-sized jars with cork tops. And in those jars is what looks like disembodied limbs and organs swimming in a translucent yellow liquid. Heads, hands, what looks to be a heart and a brain.

Each jar has a neatly written label dated a week apart, the most recent from last Monday. Is that where Grant goes on her excursions each week? To collect whatever is in these jars? It has to be.

I clench my jaw, let out something between a sob and a scream, covering my mouth with my hands. I don't understand why Grant would have this here, in her house. It feels like these creatures are stalking me in the dark, crawling all over my body and making it itch. I climb back on to the window ledge and steady myself like a tightrope walker. I can't jump, but I can lower my body down.

Closing the window behind me I take a few deep breaths in the wind to calm me, before hanging from the ledge so my feet are just a couple of metres from the ground. Then I drop down, landing hard. But still my chest feels tight, and no matter how much I try to gulp in air it doesn't loosen.

The warmth that meets me as I step back into the kitchen should be inviting, but all I see now are eyeballs and frayed limbs beyond the hidden door. My whole body is shaking, though I'm not sure if it's because of the cold or what I saw in the storeroom.

As I tiptoe upstairs, back to my room, Amélie stands by the open door of the bathroom, a beam of moonlight shining down on her as she watches my movements.

I put a finger to my lips. *Don't tell*, I try to communicate to her as I close my door behind me.

Amélie hops away, down the stairs, to return to her bed in front of the secret door.

CHAPTER 16

The fireflies arrive at just past four in the morning on Monday. I wonder if they come then because they know Grant is asleep. I'm not sure why they're afraid of her but I wonder if it has something to do with the jars in her storeroom.

I have summer school in a few hours and only the birds are awake, chirping cheerily outside my window. I slept badly. My breathing feels heavy, like something is sitting on my chest, and every time I close my eyes I see the contents of the jars. The eyes watching me, the limbs reaching for me. When I drift off I imagine, somehow, that I've shrunk to the size of a butterfly and I've been put in a jar, preserved for all time. Except then I'm standing in the cupboard watching myself, and I see my arms floating in the yellow-green water, my hair fanning around me, eyes closed, bubbles escaping my lips as I gasp for air.

And then I start shivering and pull the covers close, wanting to hide away.

It's as if the fireflies have been watching all night, waiting for me to open my eyes before slipping through the cracks of the door. They guide me down the hall, into Grant's library. I walk past her desk, where papers are lined up neatly and books stacked in order of size beside them.

There's a big gap in her shelf where she's pulled books out, ready to return them when she's done reading them. Through the gap I see tree branches reach out, stopping just short of Grant's desk. They form a little seat for me, and the fireflies land on either side of it, one by one. I step forward and sit on the branches, watching the room shrink away as they pull me through the shelves into the firefly forest beyond.

The forest is bigger this time, or perhaps I'm further in. I can't tell.

Before, when I knocked on the trees for hours and hours, I managed to cover the whole forest, from one side to the other. But now that would be impossible. There's nothing but trees for miles and miles, and I can't see where they end. If the fireflies sent me on the same quest today, I'd fail and be stuck here forever.

It's quiet, and I can hear the same birdsong that had come from Grant's garden. But then I feel the forest floor vibrate, and the birds flap their wings frantically before flying away. They hear it before I do: the familiar clip-clop, and the howling of wind like an animal's cry.

I'm tired, my eyes blurry with sleep, and so it takes me a while to see that the horseman is galloping towards me. Each blink and he's closer, closing in. Everything feels like it's happening in slow motion, my senses lagging behind. I expect him to snatch me up, take me to the underwater lair that Ruby described in her presentation, or to slam his axe down again. But instead he stops in front of me, the horse's mane blowing in the wind.

It's so close I can feel its hot breath, hear its lungs rise and fall. The horse's legs reach above my shoulders and its body, with the horseman looming on top of it, is even taller.

The horse dips its head down, snuffling around one pocket of my dressing gown, as if it wants something from it. I reach in, and feel my hand surround something waxy, followed by dripping juice. The apple the fireflies rejected last time, chewed by Amélie.

I hold the apple in front of me like an offering, and the horse munches it from my outstretched palm, its whiskers tickling my skin. It seems this was the right thing to do, because instead of slamming his axe down again, the horseman speaks for the first time.

Make your request, Hazel Al-Otaibi, he says, his voice reverberating through the trees.

His voice comes from the place where his mouth would be, if he had a face, and I peer up at his imaginary eyes.

'Do you know anything about a . . . a key?' I ask, clearing my throat nervously. Following the fireflies is like reading a book where I'm the only one who doesn't know the story.

I am the keeper of the keys, says the horseman. He speaks like he's reciting a well-known script, rehearsed and performed many times before. *And I hold the skeleton key.*

'Skeleton key?' I repeat, thinking of a key carved from bone.

I want to ask him more but I'm not sure a headless man who just tried to murder me with an axe is going to answer my questions.

I will give you the key you seek if you do me a favour in return.

'Oh, well, I –'

But he continues before I can finish speaking, in the same automatic tone. *Seek out the wolf and ask him for a horseshoe made of brass. Bring the horseshoe and I'll trade it for a key.*

I frown. 'A horseshoe?' Then I look down and see the horse holding one leg up above the ground. 'I thought you'd ask for a head.'

Why would I ask for one of those? the horseman replies, sounding curious, amused.

'Oh, I . . . no reason. Yes, OK, I'll get you a horseshoe,'

I say before I have the chance to think about what I'm agreeing to, because I want to help the horse and I'd rather keep my limbs intact by not angering the horseman. But as the horse and rider step away and disappear into the gloom, my mind turns to how to collect the horseshoe from the wolf.

When I saw the horseman today he tried to slam his axe down on me, until I fed his horse. An offering. But I have no more apples and I doubt the wolf eats apples anyway. How will it react when we meet?

As the firefly forest spits me out into Grant's library room, I realise there's a pattern. The next time I enter the forest the wolf will be waiting. And I'll have to ask it for a favour.

CHAPTER 17

'Let's start by getting into pairs,' Ms Basra says a few hours later, during our lesson.

After returning from the firefly forest I looked up Grant's jars online. They look a lot like specimen jars, which the Victorians used to preserve living things. I'm not that surprised because Grant sort of looks like a Victorian person to me, so does her house.

How old are these specimens, I wonder? *And how old is Grant?*

She has grey hair and wrinkles on her face that tell stories of a life well-lived, but when I look at photos of her with Dad from when he was my age (she has them dotted round the house), she looks exactly the same. Same clothes and hair and everything.

'Well?' Ruby says, pulling her table closer to mine. 'Are we pairing up, or what?'

It's pretty obvious that we're going to pair up, as Ezra and Akin are already friends, and we're . . . Well, I guess we're friendly.

'Sorry.' I yawn. 'I didn't sleep well.' I don't offer further explanation, but luckily I don't need to with Ruby.

'Don't worry, I slept very well and I already know what I want to do, so . . .' she shrugs, 'if you're happy for me to take the lead, I can just get started.'

'The lead on what?' I ask, confused.

Ruby raises her eyebrows and smirks, pointing at the board, just as Ms Basra starts speaking again.

'We've spent a bit of time talking about fairy-tale settings, and we'll return to those again next lesson, but I want us to spend some time now thinking about our characters. Because your character can impact your setting. So I'm going to assign each pair a different character who might appear in a fairy tale, and I want you to add them to your word bank. We'll share our word banks at the end of the lesson and see if we come up with similarities.'

I watch as Ms Basra writes an assortment of different words around a cloud with 'characters' written in it in capital letters. She has neat writing that curls and whirls like vines wrapping around a tree. She starts with: witch, dragon, prince, before turning to us for more suggestions.

'Wolf,' I say almost immediately. 'Like in Little Red Riding Hood.'

'That's a good one!' Ruby grins at me, and I watch as her eyes slip downwards to my hands. They're covered in scratches and grazes and I pull my cardigan sleeve over to hide the evidence of the fireflies' visits.

'Why have you only written prince?' Ezra asks, putting his hand up at first before realising he doesn't need to. 'What about princesses?'

Ms Basra raises her eyebrows and smiles. 'That's a good question. I want you all to think about the role of princes and princesses, and why they are the way they are . . . And, most importantly, if there's room to change that. Do princes always need to be the ones doing the rescuing? Ezra, I'd like you and Akin to present your word bank for this category.'

Ezra nods, but Akin glares at him. I hear him mutter, 'I wanted to do wolf – that's much more fun!'

I think about the very real wolf I'm supposedly meant to approach in the forest, and think that it doesn't sound fun when you're living the story.

'I love witches,' Ruby declares confidently when Ms Basra asks us what we want to study and I nod in agreement, hoping she'll forget the scratches on my hands.

Soon we're scribbling away on our own, while Ms Basra reads a book at the front. She's also munching on some of the matcha butter biscuits Ruby brought in. We each take turns to bring in a treat. I'm last. I was going to ask Grant to help me, but the way things are at the moment I feel a bit awkward.

'OK, I've already thought about this,' Ruby continues, jumping in right away. 'And there are loads of different witches in fairy tales.' She hardly takes a breath as she lists them, tapping each finger on her right hand as she does. There is, according to Ruby, the sea witch in The Little Mermaid who steals the mermaid's voice in exchange for power, the witch in Rapunzel who traps her in a tower, and the one in Hansel and Gretel who lures them to her gingerbread house, only to bake them in her oven.

'She what?' I ask, horrified. In Dad's version they all lived happily ever after, eating lots of sweet treats. I tell Ruby this.

'Oh yeah, well, if you read the *actual* fairy tales, not the ones they show in films and stuff, they're much creepier.'

I think back to how Dad calls Grant's house the gingerbread house, and I think about Grant's storeroom of weird things in jars. Is Grant some sort of witch? But why, then, would my parents send me here on my own? Why would they send me here *at all*?

Unless they're trying to get rid of you. My deepest, darkest fear comes crawling to the surface.

As Ruby explains the story – the woodsman sends his children away because he can no longer feed them – I feel a little like my parents have sent me away for their own reasons.

'Anyway,' Ruby interrupts my worries. 'I guess cannibalism is a little too dark for our word bank, huh?'

'Erm,' I say, feeling a little sick. 'Maybe.'

We spend some time thinking about words and deciding which ones to include.

'What about curse?' Ruby suggests. 'There's often some kind of curse, like the mermaid's voice being taken away from her.'

'In Rapunzel,' I say, thinking back to the apple I took from the firefly forest, 'she's taken from her parents as a punishment because they stole food from the witch's garden when her mother was pregnant with her . . .'

'Yes, good one!' Ruby says, and I feel like maybe I'm finally settling in at summer school. If only things were as easy at home.

I still don't understand why Grant would want the jars in her house. In Practical Biology last Friday, we did a virtual tour of a botanical garden in London. It had a butterfly house and tropical flowers, all preserved in this great big room. That's how we observe the natural world now, not trapping it in jars . . .

As I try and piece together this information with what we learned today, I can't help but wonder:

Is Grant really a witch? Is that why the fireflies are afraid of her? And if she is, am I cursed and should *I* be afraid of her too?

CHAPTER 18

'What sorts of things make you think of witches?'
Ruby asks.

We're sitting at Grant's kitchen table a few days after
our last lesson. Grant is pottering around the kitchen,
listening while Ruby and I work on our project. Grant is
a constant presence – sipping tea, moving cutlery around,
running the tap – and each noise grates on me a little. I'm
more on edge than usual.

'Biscuits with your tea?' Grant asks, interrupting, offering
a tin of mixed biscuits which she places on the table.

Ever since I opened the door to Grant's secret storeroom
things have been weird between us, and ever since I snuck
in through the window (not that she knows anything about
that), it's become even more awkward on my part. I don't
know how to talk to her. It feels like there's this chasm of

unspoken words separating us more and more. I have so much I WANT to ask her but I just don't know how to go about doing it. I'm glad, today, to have Ruby with me as a buffer.

'Oh, thank you,' Ruby says, accepting a bourbon biscuit gratefully. I watch as Ruby peels each side apart, licks the chocolate, and then places the biscuit back together before dipping it in her tea, leaving chocolate crumbs behind.

'It tastes weird,' I say, when I try to do the same thing myself. The chocolate is a little chalky, and I don't want to swallow the crumbs or spit them out, so I stick my tongue out instead hoping to release the taste back into the world.

That makes Ruby laugh, which makes me happy. 'Here, try this one instead,' she says, picking up a Jammy Dodger, which is round with a heart shape cut into it. I like that one better because the texture of the jam is smooth, and the biscuit melts in my mouth.

'Right,' Ruby says, wiping the crumbs from her hands. 'Let's start by looking at our wordbank. What words have you got on your list?'

'Erm,' I say, flicking through the mess of papers in my bag. 'I can't find it.'

'Shall I start?' says Ruby, with a grin.

'Yes, please!' I answer at once. *Get a grip, Hazel*, I add, only to myself. It annoys me how disorganised I am at the moment.

Usually I'm much more prepared for things, especially as the eldest cousin. I miss what I'm like when the fireflies aren't around, sucking out all my energy and taking over my mind. Between them and moving, and the mystery of Grant's storeroom, my brain feels like an overflowing cup.

Ruby pulls out her notebook, neatly titled 'Summer School' with her name beneath it, and flicks through a few pages quickly. I still manage to spot all of the writing and research she's done – turning her notes into a scrapbook of sorts. Eventually she lands on a double spread with the title 'Fairy Tale Word Bank'. There are words like *forest* and *leaves* and *dark*; and then other words like *three* and *spell*.

'Why did you write three?' I ask, determined to contribute a little more.

'Oh!' Ruby says. 'Well in fairy tales things often happen in threes. Three quests, three pigs, three bears . . .'

As Ruby continues listing things, I think of the three fireflies, and the creatures in the forest. There's the headless horseman, and the wolf . . . Does that mean I'll meet a third? I hope it's not a bear, like Ruby said. Or a dragon. Now that I think about everything we've studied in summer school so far, the firefly forest is a bit like a fairy tale. And fairy tales have patterns and rules and . . .

'Morals,' I say to Ruby, adding my own word. 'All fairy tales have them. It's why Rapunzel was taken – to teach a moral about stealing.'

Like the fireflies are doing with me.

Ruby nods, scribbling it down. 'What's our moral, then?' she asks.

'I'm not sure . . . Maybe we can decide later?' I suggest, wanting to find my own moral, because I can't help but disagree with the fireflies even as I obey them. 'Once we've done our mood board?'

Ruby nods. 'Good idea. It would be good if we came up with our own, rather than using one from another story.'

I feel like I'm slowly starting to understand the work we're doing. It took me a while to catch up – I grew up learning different stories.

'So the last word you've written down is "spell",' I say. 'And we all know witches cast spells but what sorts of spells should we explore?'

'I quite like incantations,' says Ruby. 'So maybe we could come up with a rhyme that's a spell?'

'Hmmm.' I think about this for a bit. The quest I've been sent on by the fireflies is all because of the stolen apple.

'What about enchantments?' says Grant, interrupting again.

'Yes!' says Ruby excitedly, adding it to the mood board. 'That's a great word. And it works with curses, which we decided on during our last lesson.'

'It's all to do with pagan magic,' continues Grant.

'Curses and enchantments.' I watch as she chops apples into thin slices, mixing them with sugar and cinnamon before laying them on top of some pastry.

As I watch Grant's hands move swiftly, Ruby asks question after question. 'What's pagan magic?'

'It involves the natural world. Using herbs, and other items from your garden,' Grant explains, placing her pie in the oven now. 'We could collect some leaves and flowers from the garden for your mood board, if you like?'

I haven't been into Grant's garden since she saw me look through the secret door. And I'd really like to explore again, find more bugs for my book, and learn about flowers too. So Ruby and I happily agree.

Five minutes later we're standing by the window I nearly fell off when I snuck into Grant's storeroom.

'My mother gave me my first jasmine seed,' Grant explains as we pick flowers and pass them to her. 'It's funny because it comes from your part of the world,' she says, glancing at me. 'And yet, here it is, like you.'

I think Grant is trying to be nice, but I wonder if she regrets letting me stay with her. Has Dad ever seen the secret room? Maybe it didn't exist when he lived here. Either way, her words create more of a distance between us. Sometimes our differences feel as stark as night and day and I can't find any common ground.

'I'm sure we can spare one flower,' Grant says, plucking it delicately. 'And spread the petals over your mood board.'

After that, Grant opens the garden gate and we collect all manner of branches, leaves and flowers – ivy, peonies, rose thorns. Grant is being nice, gentle, just as she was before, and I wonder if maybe I judged her too harshly. Of course there's nothing to be afraid of. I just wish I understood what was in those jars and why she keeps them locked up.

'WAIT!' says Ruby suddenly, and I stop as I'm about to step forward, my foot hovering in the air.

'What?' I ask, alarmed. But Ruby's not looking at me, she's ducked down under my shoe.

'A snail!' Ruby picks it up from the path and holds it up to my eye. It has a swirly white shell, which it is completely hidden inside. 'You nearly stepped on it.'

'Good spot, Ruby,' said Grant. 'Stepping on a snail would be bad luck, especially for the snail! But finding one brings good fortune.'

'Really?' I ask.

Grant nods. 'Most gardeners I know hate slugs and snails, because they eat all sorts of plants. But I think it's about learning to live in harmony, and realising that this garden doesn't belong to us, but to every creature living in it.'

All I know about snails is that a group of them is called

a route. I tell Grant and Ruby this and they seem pleased.

Ruby gently places the snail on the flower bed, and we keep going. I'm careful, now, to respect all the living creatures here while Grant points out her different plants and flowers, some of which she'd already shown me. I stand back as she pulls Ruby in with her knowledge, and I see how her face comes to life.

'Hazel!' Grant says in a loud whisper waving me over with one hand while pointing at a peony with another. 'See that?'

I see a red body with several spots and six legs. 'A ladybird!' I reply, and I think how beautiful it is.

'The red ones always have seven spots, did you know?' Grant explains. 'They're good luck too. If ever one lands on you, you should make a wish and sing the rhyme:

> *Ladybird, ladybird, fly away home,*
> *Your house is on fire, your children are gone.*

'In fact, there's so much in this garden that marks luck, if you look it up. And I truly believe in it. Fortune. Working with it, passing it along.'

'Like a real witch,' Ruby says, and I turn to her, surprised. But then I realise she means it in a good way.

'Exactly,' Grant says, and I can see she's pleased by Ruby's comment. She explains to us that many witches were actually healers, and they used medicinal herbs to help their towns. 'They're often misunderstood. Old, unmarried women like me. But the best people, I think, don't always fit the mould.'

Something about Grant's words burrows into my soul, warming it. Moving here I was so worried about being different, because of my accent and the way I look; and the fireflies always made me feel strange and weird. So did my interest in collective nouns and bugs. But maybe all of those things make me unique.

'What's a group of ladybirds called, Hazel?' Ruby asks, and I'm pleased she's turning to me for information.

'A loveliness,' I say, grinning. It's one of the kindest collective nouns, I think, but seeing a ladybird up close I can see why they're called that.

The ladybird flies away just then, as if to pass on its luck to someone else.

Back inside, Ruby and I begin to glue everything we've foraged on to our mood board, and suddenly I have an extra special idea.

'What if we make it like a maze?' I suggest. 'With something at the centre, like . . . like an apple.' I realise this sounds very similar to the quests the fireflies have been setting me. But maybe they can spark inspiration as well as misery . . .

'That's a brilliant idea!' Ruby says. 'Maybe our story

could have a maze too.'

We find a trail online and trace it out, before sticking all of the foliage round it. Ruby struggles with this bit, accidentally gluing her fingers together and breaking a few leaves and flowers. So, for once, I get to teach her something and properly contribute.

The maze reminds me of the snail out in the garden, and the trail of slime it had left across the path. If the apple was the only thing that saved me from the horseman's attack, I feel certain I'm going to need some sort of good luck charm to face the wolf.

'It's a work of art!' says Grant, when we're done. 'I think you've both earned a slice of pie.' She sets a tray down on the table. It's warm from the oven, heat steaming from it.

Apple pie. Like the poisoned apple in Snow White. Like the witch who fed Hansel and Gretel in her gingerbread house. Like the apple I stole from the fireflies and Amélie took a bite from.

'I like Grant,' whispers Ruby, gratefully accepting a slice with some custard.

I wonder if there's more to Grant's story than I first thought. She has strange jars locked away in a storeroom, but the fireflies seemed to be repelled by her. That can only be a good thing, can't it? Does she have something to do with the firefly forest? She seems to weave into it in ways I don't understand. Like Grant and Ruby said earlier, witches are misunderstood, so maybe I've done the same with her.

The pie tastes good, the sweetness and sourness blending in my mouth, the pastry crumbling. It warms my belly as I swallow. While I eat and work with my new friend, I'm able to forget the fireflies' quests and demands, even if for just a moment.

CHAPTER 19

It's Akin's turn to bring in treats this Monday. We crowd around him when he enters the room with a big shopping bag stacked high with containers.

'I got some puff-puff,' Akin says, which he explains is a deep-fried dough, for those of us who haven't had it before.

'Oh, bless *you*,' says Ms Basra, more excited than the rest of us.

Akin glows at this as he lays the food out on the table.

'Did your mum make some more puff-puff?' Ezra says as soon as he walks in. 'YES!' he says, holding his hands up like a miracle's just occurred. Then he turns to Ruby and me and explains that Akin's mum is the best cook he's ever met.

'Yeah, but your mum just makes ready meals,' Akin replies, and Ezra laughs.

'That's why we always sleepover at *your* house.'

We chatter for a bit, while Ms Basra finishes setting up her workspace, and I feel a strange warmth wash over me. I know three people in my new class next year, and it turns out we're all going to be in Ms Basra's form! I'm not sure if she had anything to do with it, but it makes the whole starting a new school thing seem a little less scary.

I'm now well settled into my routine, but things still surprise me each day: like everyone has very different accents to one another, some I find harder to understand; and people here walk everywhere, whereas in Kuwait everyone drives.

'We'll have to have Grant's apple pie at *our* sleepover,' Ruby whispers, and I think that sounds like a fun idea. Maybe *that's* what I can make when it's my turn to bring in treats!

Soon after, Ms Basra makes us move the desks out of the way so we can have a bit of a stage at the front to set up our mood boards. She pulls out an artist's easel. We're meant to go up in our pairs, and present our mood board together for a few minutes while talking through our inspiration.

After we have presented, Ms Basra says we can spend the rest of the day doing whatever we like to celebrate being halfway through summer school, so Ezra has brought in his Switch and some extra controllers, and Ms Basra is going to let us set it up and play against each other.

'I've also ordered pizza for lunch!' she declares. 'So let's save the puff-puff for dessert.'

Ezra and Akin end up going first, and they suddenly look nervous, dragging their board forward to discuss their theme. They talk about princes and castles, so their mood board has lots of printed photos of old castles, while they discuss various rescue attempts made in fairy tales.

Ms Basra, Ruby and I clap when they're done.

'When you were given your character,' Ms Basra says, holding a pen to her mouth while she thinks up questions, 'you asked me about princesses. After doing research for your mood board what conclusion did you come to?'

Akin turns to Ezra, eyebrows raised, as if to say 'you're the reason we have to answer this, so you do it'.

Ezra fumbles a little, clearly taken off guard by the question, which I guess isn't part of what they've rehearsed, and I suddenly feel a wave of nerves wash over me about having to answer one too. Ruby has written our script out carefully in neatly joined-up writing, and we agreed to stick to it exactly.

'I . . . Well . . .' says Ezra, turning red.

'It's OK,' says Ms Basra kindly. 'Take your time.'

Ezra takes a deep breath, pauses, and then he speaks, not looking at anyone in particular.

'Well, the thing is, I noticed a lot of the stories have princes saving princesses, which is fine, I guess, to have that once or twice, but I found it a bit boring that they were *all* like that.'

Ms Basra nods, a barely disguised grin on her face.

'And if *you* were going to write your own fairy tale, what do you think you would do?'

Ezra seems less nervous about this question. 'I, well . . . I guess I would try it the other way around.'

Akin pulls a face just then, and turns to Ezra. 'Why does it have to be princes and princesses anyway? Why can't it be something different . . .?'

Ezra seems confused. 'Like what?' he asks.

Akin shrugs. 'Maybe, I dunno. Like *The Avengers* except in a fairy tale.'

Ruby giggles at that.

'That's a *wonderful* idea!' says Ms Basra, encouragingly. 'I think you've all done enough research now, so it's time to start writing your fairy tales together in your pairs. But in the way Ezra and Akin have shown here – bring your own twist to it.' She says this to me and Ruby now. 'While fairy tales are a great source material, the world has changed since they were first written, and so I want you to write with *your* interests front and centre, whether that be superheroes, or animals, or cars . . .'

As Ms Basra continues to explain, Ruby scribbles down her instructions in her summer school notebook. I can't help but think of *my* story – the one I'm living.

And I realise I'm starting to want to share it, rather than hide it away like a secret.

It's mine and Ruby's turn to present now. Nerves fizz through my body all the way to my fingertips. I understand, now, how Ezra and Akin must've felt a few moments ago. It's like I could zap electricity from them if I tried. My breathing is heavy too, though I don't think that's the nerves because it's been like this for a while. Every morning I wake up with a heaviness in my chest, my breathing slightly wheezy. It gets worse during Practical Biology, when we roam the school grounds outside, or after I've been in Grant's garden.

Ruby carries our mood board carefully to the front, and I follow behind, trying to gulp down extra air, as if it'll help. When I turn, I see Akin and Ezra are looking at the board, not at me, and they seem impressed by our display. It looks like a living, breathing forest on paper. The flowers and leaves and branches are all bunched together, with the maze weaving through them. I even gathered some small rocks after Ruby left the other night and stuck them down to make it seem like a *real* path. Then I got a bit carried away and drew snails and ladybirds and a pond right at the centre of the maze. I was worried Ruby would hate it but she was thrilled and said that I'm going to be 'the best artist in our year' when school begins.

As I think of that, and see Akin's and Ezra's impressed

faces, I feel a little less nervous, though my palms are still sweating, so I have to grip tight to the cards I'll be reading from.

'Our theme is witches,' begins Ruby, her voice loud and clear. 'After analysing our word bank, we came up with the word "enchantment". There are many of those in fairy tales. For example, the poisoned apple in Snow White . . .'

Ruby continues to list examples of enchantments, and I wait until it's my turn to speak.

When Ruby falls silent it's my turn.

'W-we,' I begin, then quickly clear my throat because I make a sound like a frog's croak. 'We decided that instead of pictures . . .' I pause, focusing on the words on my card, 'we would go into the garden and collect lots of different herbs and flowers as examples of the type of ingredients witches in fairy tales would have used.'

I take a deep breath when I'm done with my bit, but my face feels hot and my chest feels tight.

Ruby goes on to list the ingredients and their properties, including jasmine, lavender and rose petals.

'A lot of witch's houses are always at the centre of a great big forest,' I say. 'They can be difficult to find, hidden in the trees, so we decided to draw a maze with leaves surrounding it. And we wondered whether anyone would like to come up and try the maze?'

A pause, with Akin and Ezra turning to one another, before they both put their hands up.

I grin, relieved.

'What a *wonderful* idea,' says Ms Basra. 'Well done. All right, as it wouldn't be fair to pick between Akin and Ezra . . . I think it'll just have to be me! I *love* mazes.'

In the end, Akin and Ezra come up and help her complete it, and we all cheer when she gets to the centre. Suddenly, I don't feel nervous any more, just really relieved and proud.

'Now,' says Ms Basra, turning serious again. 'You've done such a wonderful job, especially with the maze, that I won't ask you a question, but I *will* ask you to ponder this as you come to write your stories: how are witches portrayed in fairy tales, and what do you think *you* could do to change the way they're represented? A big question, I know, but I believe in both of you. I want you to put a hint of yourselves in the story.'

When we're done and start celebrating our halfway-through-summer-school day, I think about Ms Basra's words.

I've put my whole self into the forest, into the story unwinding in front of me. But, just like my life, I feel like I'm following a path set for me by everyone else – my parents, the fireflies. Can I really change it, the way Ms Basra is suggesting?

Maybe. A quiet, confident voice springs from the back of my mind, reminding me of the trees as they defend me from the dangers of the fireflies' quest.

CHAPTER 20

I'm in a different part of the firefly forest this time.
One minute I was foraging in Grant's garden for a lucky snail shell, and the next, as I exited the gate with my findings clasped in my palm, instead of her house I found the firefly forest. The branches grow thicker here, each one scratching at my face and arms, grabbing at my clothes and hair. I hear a low rumbling coming from beneath their roots, like a growling cat. It releases into the air like a hiss of warning.

The fireflies have disappeared somewhere in the depths of the forest. They came to collect me and now they've left me here to complete my mission: seek out the wolf.

The ground is soft, swamplike, and I'm glad I'm in shoes and proper clothes, not my dressing gown and slippers.

Eventually I manage to free myself from the branches,

though it feels as if they're trying to stop me, trying to drag me back from the path I've taken. I can feel the trees' hearts beating, drumming faster than my hurried steps, but they don't speak to me like the fireflies. I can just sense their worries floating in the air around me, like dandelions on a breezy day.

Soon I trip, and I look down, head torch on, to find a great big paw print. It looks like a dog's, but it's much bigger, so big that both of my feet fit inside, with room to spare. And I know I'm on the path to the wolf. I follow its giant steps, hand wrapped around the snail shell, glad I managed to pluck it just in time. I think about Hansel and Gretel and the breadcrumb trail. Will this path lead me to the ending that Dad told me about – where they all live happily ever after? Or will my story end with me gobbled up whole?

Very soon, I can hear the now-familiar clip-clop of hooves to my right. The horseman is here with me, in this strange new part of the forest. He doesn't approach this time. Perhaps he won't until I have what he needs, but at least now he wants something from me he won't hurt me. There are rules in the forest, I'm realising. And I'm no longer navigating it mapless, with nothing but the fireflies' whims to guide me. I'm starting to find my own path.

I walk and walk for what seems like hours until I eventually reach a cluster of rocks. Hidden behind them, with vines covering its entrance, is a cave. The wolf's prints stop abruptly, so I know it must be inside.

Now I'm here I'm frozen to the spot. Flies buzz around the cave door, surrounding skeletal remains. I slow down my approach but keep moving, trying hard not to breathe the sourness of it, not to take in the evil that lurks beyond that entrance.

Are you lost? a voice hisses. I look round, unsure of where it has come from, when up ahead on the uppermost rock I see two shining eyes, like fireflies, attached to a ginormous brown-grey body.

A wolf. *The* wolf. It watches me, looming larger as it leaps down from rock to rock. I try to move but my feet are stuck to the ground. I can't tell if it's the mud, or my fear. My body is a hive, hot and cold at once, and I no longer feel my limbs. I feel more like a puppet, about to tumble to the floor with no one to hold me up. As the wolf moves closer and closer, its paws squelching in the mud, I grip the snail shell in my palm, careful not to break it.

I try to speak, to make my request, but the words come out strangled, like something is pushing against my throat.

Good, the wolf says in response to my silence. *I prefer my lunch to be quiet.*

My breath feels heavy too with the same wheezy-sharp pain in my chest. Up closer, the wolf's full height on all fours becomes apparent. It is taller than me, each of its legs reaching up to my shoulders like the horse. Its fur smells sharp, tangy, the smell of rot.

'I –' I begin, hoping that by making my request I might distract it. But the wolf interrupts.

What's that in your hand? It's definitely speaking, though its mouth doesn't move; it's like a too-real ventriloquist puppet, watching me with hungry eyes.

I open my palm and the snail's shell shines bright. The wolf's expression changes. Instead of looking pleased at the offering, the way the headless horseman had, it looks angry and, perhaps, a little afraid.

A deep growl builds up in the wolf's throat, before it speaks again.

How dare you bring this to my doorstep.

'I-I didn't mean to, I –'

Leave, growls the wolf. *Now. Or next time I see you I'll swallow you whole.*

My whole body is shaking – I don't understand. I need to make my request, need to ask for the horseshoe. But the wolf is different to the horseman; it chomps and bites at the words stuck in my throat, and I don't think any offering will soften the look of hatred in its eyes.

Or is it fear?

Finally, my legs start to work, though I wobble when I move. I take a step back, and the wolf doesn't follow – it's like it can't reach me. And I wonder if it's to do with the snail being lucky, the way Grant had said. Or maybe because it's taken from her garden – something from the person the fireflies fear. Either way, it seems to have saved me.

I take another step and the wolf stands still, pacing from side to side like an invisible wall is holding it back. At the third step I trip over something hard in the swamp, a tree root maybe, and the snail shell tumbles out of my hands and into the mud.

The wolf's eyes widen, like he's won a prize, and I pull myself up, now caked in mud. *That was a very silly mistake you just made,* he says. Saliva drips from his jaws. *Don't worry, this won't take long . . .*

A split second passes, and then something inside me, something innate, something hundreds of years old passed down to me from my ancestors, tells me to run.

As I race through the mud, splashing my legs and trying hard not to slip, I can hear the wolf's driving paws just behind me, feel his hot breath on the back of my neck.

I'm struggling to breathe, my chest getting tighter, like needles are poking at it. Any moment and he'll topple me to the floor and gobble me up. I manage, somehow, to reach the brambles, and from behind me I hear the wolf squeal.

I take a risk and turn to see the trees have created a tall fence, covered in thorns, stopping him from crossing. Now I know why they were holding me back earlier: they were protecting me.

Even with the distance between us, I run and run until I'm back in Grant's garden and go all the way up the stairs into my room. Once I've settled, warmed up again and stopped shaking, I see that I've left a trail of muddy footprints caking their way up the stairs, and I spend half the night, while Grant is asleep, cleaning them up so the wolf can't trace them and follow me home.

CHAPTER 21

Last night I failed.

But I'm not giving up. I have to get the key, I just *have* to. I've still not managed to speak to Mama and Dad and even their emails are getting shorter and less frequent. I'm sure it's the fireflies doing this to punish me, especially after everything with the wolf.

To get the key I need to face the wolf again and ask him for the horseshoe. Only then will the headless horseman help me. The snail shell seemed to work to protect me, so maybe that's what I need: a little bit of luck on my side to fight my curse. Or a *lot*. Not just one snail shell, but a group of them, to surround the wolf and force it to do my bidding.

The next few days pass slowly and uneventfully. The clouds

are overcast, leaving a dull, gloomy haze on everything, and the house is cold even though it's summer. It rains on and off for a few days, and everything smells a little damp. I'm not at summer school today and because she can't be out in her garden, Grant works at her desk while I sit a few metres from her in the same room with the TV on, filling in my workbook for Art.

I've managed to combine all of my classes: drawing bugs and leaves in Art that I've found for Practical Biology. And as I learn the properties of each of them I share them with Ruby, picking details that will be relevant to our story.

Grant, apparently, can focus even if 'a live orchestra is performing around me', so she doesn't mind me being there. Things are a bit better after Ruby visited and we went round Grant's garden, but I still haven't managed to figure out what is in her storeroom. I've tried to ask her about it twice, but each time she changes the subject. I'm no longer afraid of the jars, because I'm sure they're why the fireflies are afraid of Grant. And if I could figure out why and how, maybe I can stop the fireflies for good. But only *after* I finish this one last quest, and stop my deepest, darkest fear from coming true.

Right now, I have the TV on in the background while painting the firefly forest, with its brown-red furry bark and long, twisting branches. I'm taking it slow, focusing on each tree at a time, each nook and bump and scar it holds. Something about painting makes me feel comforted.

Amélie sits by my side – she's shaking and seems extra jumpy.

'Rabbits can sense a change in weather,' says Grant, when I ask her what's wrong. 'Before a big storm, they usually go and hide in a forest.'

I frown at the thought of this. In a forest? There aren't any nearby, as far as I know. The land around here is flat and full of fields. So where else could Amélie hide but the firefly forest? After all, if I can take the apple out of it and the snail shell into it, she must be able to go in too.

Still, there's one good thing about the rain: it brings snails with it. I'm going to meet Ruby later in a field just across the street from school to go snail-shell collecting. It's funny, because I didn't expect her to say yes, but I said, in return, I'd be her goalkeeper for when she needs to practise hockey.

Lots more kids signed up to sports at summer school than the other subjects. I've never really done any sport before, so I didn't pick one, and now I'm glad because it's raining most of the time. Whenever I see Ruby outside during my Art lessons, she's always covered in mud, waving her hockey stick at me with a grin.

I find my first snail shell on the way to meet her, and something about it – glinting at me like a jewel – makes me feel safe. Like I can't come to any harm with it by my side.

Soon after, Ruby waves at me from the field – raincoat and wellies on.

'So one thing I didn't ask,' she says, jumping immediately into conversation as soon as we meet, 'is why you're collecting snail shells in the first place.'

For a moment I'm tempted to say it's for Practical Biology, but I decide to test the waters, wondering if it's the right time to tell her. I explain that the snail shells make me feel safe from harm, and to my surprise Ruby grins.

'It's like they're your magic talisman.'

'I've heard of those,' I say, thinking about various video games I've played with Omar. 'But what exactly are they meant to do?'

'Protect you . . . Actually, you know this could actually be a *really* cool idea for our fairy tale . . .'

As Ruby talks, I'm aware of how long it's been since I last saw the fireflies: four days.

Today is the first day I can't see the scratch marks they leave behind on my hands each time they visit. But almost as soon as the fireflies enter my mind, they appear in front of me. Scratch, scratch, scratching my skin. Ruby doesn't notice, of course, but I pull my sleeves over my hands.

How can I leave now, without telling her what's going on? But then, maybe I don't have to keep this a secret after all? Maybe this would be the perfect time to tell her, especially as she understood why I want the snail shells . . .

'Are you OK?' Ruby's staring at me now, looking worried. I suppose she can see how I keep hiding my hands in my sleeves, and I suppose if I don't tell her now, anything else I explain will sound weirder.

'I –' I sigh. 'I need to tell you something.'

Ruby purses her lips and gives me her full attention. Our snail hunt is abandoned, with a solitary snail shell in my hands.

'There are these fireflies . . .' I begin hurriedly, while the fireflies flit around my face and pull at my clothes. One of them crawls into my ponytail, and I want so much to shake my head around, to pull my scrunchy off, but I don't think it would help me explain this all to Ruby. 'They turn up randomly, sort of. Or when I'm feeling stressed, I guess. They're here right now.'

Ruby frowns, peering around as if trying to see them. I explain that no one else *can* see them. Except Amélie, because I think animals sense things much better than humans. I tell Ruby all about the firefly forest and the monsters that lurk inside it. All the while Ruby's frown grows and grows and grows.

'So this is a . . . dream?' Ruby asks, her voice rising in a question. 'I'm confused.'

The fireflies are now scratch, scratch, scratching at my

skin, and I pull my sleeves over my hands to stop them. But they crawl up my sleeves too, tickling my arms.

'No,' I say firmly. 'They're *real*.'

Ruby's eyes widen in what I think is recognition. 'I –' She looks behind her, as if she wants to run away. 'I don't understand.'

My heart sinks. Of course she doesn't understand.

'The snail shell!' I say instead, using the one link Ruby has to the fireflies' world to try and explain it to her. 'That's why I need the talisman. For good luck. There's a wolf, and I need to collect a horseshoe from it to give to the headless horseman. But first, I need the snails to protect me.'

When it comes out of my mouth like that, I can see why Ruby's confused. None of it makes sense, not unless you've been there, experienced it the way I have.

I can feel Ruby's faith in me slip further and further away, and it's as if a physical distance is growing between us. Branches grow from the ground, creating a thorned fence neither of us can cross. Meanwhile, the fireflies scratch, scratch, scratch.

Thunder sounds from above, as if it knows what we're feeling.

'We should go,' Ruby says, her voice different, like she's speaking to a wounded animal. I don't like it. I feel as if I've now ruined one of my favourite things about moving here – my friendship with Ruby – and the fireflies scratch,

scratch, scratch even more, making my hands tingle and my stomach knot up. 'It's going to rain soon. You can come back to mine, if you like?'

'I –' I say. I want to say that I have to follow the fireflies, but Ruby doesn't understand. 'I have to go,' I say instead, and turn to run towards Grant's house. Except, instead of a road and wheat stalks like normal, there's now a thicket of trees at the edge of the field we'd been standing in, the fireflies flitting ahead.

'Hazel!' Ruby calls once, twice. But her third call is lost to the wind.

The rest is a blur. I can't tell where the field ends and the firefly forest begins. They blend together, as if they are one singular world, my only world. Then, the whispers start.

Welcome back. Welcome back. Welcome back.

It's only then that I realise, in my haste, I dropped the snail shell back at the field, and that I'm going into the firefly forest totally unprotected.

CHAPTER 22

It's raining in the forest this time, the wolf's footsteps washed away.

But the smell of death leads me to its cave, through the branches and brambles. The trees don't stop me, and while I'm grateful for a clearer path, I find myself wondering if they're mad at me for endangering them so much. Maybe they've decided they're fed up with me and they no longer want to protect me.

The further this quest goes on, the more tired I feel of it all. Perhaps the trees feel the same.

Then I reach a strange rock that looks like a giant fossil, carved with swirls. It's a giant snail shell just outside the wolf's cave! As I approach it, I notice it's *my* snail. The one I dropped. I can tell from its markings, and the fact it's in exactly the same position. Except, just like everything else in the forest – the trees, the wolf, the fireflies – it's much bigger. I see a tiny opening, just the right size for me. And I know what I need to do.

I climb inside and curl myself into the tight space. I'm just trying to figure out how to slide it along the mud when I hear the wolf's paws.

Clever, says the wolf, its voice exceedingly calm. *Very clever. I must say, I'm impressed you've returned to me.*

I take my chance now, and speak my request:

'I'm here for the horseshoe. The horseman says you have it.'

Silence. I peek out of the crack beneath the snail's shell to see the wolf's tail swish left and right. And then:

I'll give you the horseshoe, the wolf says, *in exchange for the witch's hag stone.*

I feel my heart sinking. The fireflies are sending me on a scavenger hunt of errands that grow bigger and bigger. Unless it really *is* like a fairy tale, where things happen in threes. And the witch is my last stop . . .

'Who is this witch?' I ask, not wasting time. 'Where is she?'

The wolf laughs a wheezy laugh, reminding me of my own breathing, which is getting worse and worse as the days go by. *Tread carefully, Hazel Al-Otaibi, you don't have the key just yet. Push too hard and you might find your deepest, darkest fears come true before you get the chance. Now hurry, and wait until you're next collected.*

The wolf's words send a chill down my spine. It knows the reason for my quest, which means so do the horseman and the witch. What if she doesn't agree to give me the hag stone? I decide, now, that I need to focus my efforts on the quest and stop getting distracted by Grant's secret door. It's the only way I can think of to stop the fireflies.

Eventually, I make it back to the opening of the firefly forest, dragging the shell with me for safety. As I walk through the field, the snail shell returns to its normal size again and the trees disappear. It's dark now and Ruby is gone. I tuck the snail shell inside my jacket pocket and I vow to keep it with me at all times, ready for my next journey there – when I have to face the witch.

CHAPTER 23

I dream I'm alone in the forest. A creature with heavy, puffing breaths is following me, its feet pad, pad, padding along the floor. It's humid and I'm struggling to breathe.

I stop.

The creature stops too.

I turn.

The wolf, its fangs dripping with blood, glinting in the dark. The wolf crouches, growling at me, and it becomes more difficult to breathe.

It leaps into the air and lands on my chest, knocking me to the floor. Its weight rests on me, winding me, and my breathing is short and shallow. Its paws dig into me. I feel a sharp pain in my chest.

I wake up suddenly and lean on the backboard of the bed. My back is slick with sweat, my breaths shallow.

It was a dream. It was only a dream. But then, why can I still not breathe?

'G-Grant,' I try to call, panting. It wasn't the wolf's ragged breaths I could hear, it was my own. I try to take deep breaths but they feel sharp on my chest, like the wolf's claws are digging in. I scramble out of bed, knocking into the cupboard, my skin tingling, the blood rushing to my face.

Still, I can't breathe. It feels like the wolf is there, sitting on my chest, as I pull at my neckline, desperate to find air.

'Grant,' I cry, afraid, as the world of my nightmares has collided with the real one. 'H-help.'

'Hazel?' I finally hear a voice whisper. I look up to see Grant in a white nightdress, like a ghost, hair as neat as it always is, standing at my door. The artificial light haloes her, and she squints into the room as if struggling to see me.

'I –' I say, my breaths growing shallower by the minute. 'I can't breathe!' I cry.

Grant looks just as she had when I discovered the jars behind her door. I realise now it was not anger at all, but fear.

'It's all right, darling,' she says, soothingly. 'Does it feel like there are knives in your chest when you try to breathe?'

'Yes,' I say, letting out a sob. 'I can't –'

'It's all right, my love,' she repeats. 'Try not to speak too much. You're having an asthma attack.'

Grant explains we're going to go to the hospital and that as soon as we get there everything will be OK.

'Now,' she says, eyes glinting in the darkness. 'All you need to do is concentrate on breathing.'

But I can't because I feel like I'm drowning, like a weight is on my chest, every breath shallower than the rest. It makes me panic; tears streaming down my face.

Grant guides me down the stairs, slipping her feet into her shoes, and then grabs her coat. She gathers my coat and shoes too and helps me into the back seat of the car, strapping me in before driving away down the moonlit road.

It takes us twenty minutes to reach the hospital, though the journey feels like it lasts forever. The trees watch over us as we zoom past, their branches reaching for me as if they wanted to pull me into their depths. I imagine the trees digging my grave, placing me inside it, their thorns cutting at my cheeks. And then, slowly, they cover me in dirt until it seeps into my throat and I take my last, raggedy breath.

Would I be born anew, or would my body turn to roots that grow other trees that bleed and scream into the night?

But then I remember, the trees are my friends, and I'm on the way to hospital, and Grant said everything would be OK.

The hospital is busy, even though it's the middle of the

night. The lights are impossibly bright, and the smell of it does little to help my breathing.

Grant flags down a nurse moments after we walk in. The nurse looks harried, but her face turns to me and softens. She nods and puts a finger up as if to say 'one minute'. But I don't feel as if I have a minute left – each second is like an age.

Grant guides me to one of the blue plastic seats in A&E. Next to me a baby coughs and cries, and across, a teenager holds a bloodied tissue to their nose, drops of blood down their shirt. They lock eyes with me for a moment, and I wonder what they see. A blue-lipped, frightened twelve-year-old, wide-eyed and sallow.

Then the nurse is next to me, guiding me, and everything feels like a haze. I'm taken to a curtained corner and asked to blow into a tube. My vitals are checked and I'm placed on a bed, poised upright. But I'm tired, so tired, and I want to give in to sleep. Give in to the wolf.

Then a clear plastic mask is placed over my face and I feel a cold gas seep into my mouth, hear it hiss. The nurse tells me to breathe it in.

The first breath is like the others, shallow and painful.

The second loosens, like the wolf has removed a paw from my chest.

As a minute passes and my lungs no longer rattle and wheeze, I can breathe. I can finally breathe.

Soon after, I drift off to sleep.

The wolf is gone.

And I'm safe.

For now.

CHAPTER 24

'Can you hear me?' I ask, trying to swallow down my frustration.

It's my first day in hospital, and Grant has rung Mama and Dad for me. But the hospital has bad reception and their voices crackle, their sentences fractured. The fireflies are doing this, I'm sure of it. They're reminding me I haven't yet finished my quest. At first I thought all I'd need to do is collect a key, but things are getting more complicated: a key, a horseshoe, a hag stone. When will it end?

After three, I remind myself. If I'm right about the firefly forest being like a fairy tale – and everything else that's happened there so far suggests it is – then the witch will be my final stop.

I hear Mama say, 'Your un . . . And then he picked . . . Afterwards,' followed by muffled laughter.

'W-what did you say? Sorry I ca—' That's when the line catches up with itself, and I hear Mama's words in a rush. She's telling me a story about her brother helping her pack and accidentally blocking Mama into a room. 'Oh! I think I caught that . . . Ha. Funny.'

'Hazel?' Mama says, talking over me now. We're offbeat, each interrupting each other without meaning to, each missing what the other is saying until we talk around in circles.

Eventually, we fall silent for a few awkward moments.

'So,' says Dad after a pause. 'How's summer school?'

We spend the first ten minutes of our chat with them asking about my breathing and how I'm feeling. With the oxygen and my new medication, my breathing feels back to normal. Even the heaviness in my chest has almost disappeared. Although I've been told I need to be in here for a few days, just to be sure. I could tell, when I explained all of this, that they both felt guilty for not being here with me, but Dad seemed pleased when I told him how great Grant was.

I want to tell them all about the fairy tales we're studying in English and send them photos of my art and explain my Practical Biology findings; I want to show them the mood board Ruby and I made with Grant's help. They would be proud of it. But Mama and Dad don't even know who Ruby is, let alone how awkward our last conversation was.

There's too much to say and not enough reception on the phone to say it. 'Yeah, we're writing . . . stories.'

'You're finding it boring?' Mama tries to repeat, sounding concerned.

'No! We're writing STORIES,' I snap. 'Are you listening to me?'

A sigh. 'Oh, hun, I can't hear what you're saying. Can you hear her?' Mama says to Dad.

'A little but . . . Oh no, that's the doorbell. Right, we're going to have to leave in a moment –'

'But wait, I –'

I'm interrupted by Mama and Dad chatting to each other instead of me, about various things they need to do before Mama goes away for her last work trip.

'Hello? Hello!' I say, my voice rising in frustration, ignoring the fact that some of the other kids are staring at me now.

Finally, Mama's back on the phone. 'Hello? Habibti, can you put your aunt back on the line? We want to know everything the doctor has said to make sure you're OK.'

'But we –'

'Aunt Hazel?' Dad says, thinking I've already gone.

'Hang on,' I say, gritting my teeth before handing Grant the phone. She's perched at the end of the bed and she picks it up and walks out of the ward for better reception.

I already explained how I was doing, but for some reason

they don't believe me because I'm only twelve. But *I'm* the one who had the asthma attack. If anyone's the expert it's me, but grown-ups never believe us, do they?

That morning, the doctor said my asthma (which is a lung condition that causes breathing problems) was triggered by moving to a new climate.

'The air is more humid here,' the doctor explained. 'And with the recent rainfall, you're exposed to new types of pollen you wouldn't have been before. That's why it happened so suddenly.'

'It's because of my garden,' Grant had said, and she looked really guilty.

'But I love your garden!' I had insisted. 'It's my favourite part of the house.' And it seemed, a little, like telling Grant how I felt had started to mend the crack in our relationship from when I peered through the storeroom door.

'Will it go away when she gets used to the climate?' Grant had asked, placing a hand gently on my shoulder.

'I'm afraid not,' said the doctor. 'But it should improve as she gets older. In the meantime, she's going to need to take inhalers daily, to manage her condition.'

Condition. That's what the other doctor called the firefly visits. A condition called obsessive compulsive disorder.

Soon Grant is done with the phone and the nurse returns to check my vitals and give me another dose of oxygen. I'm supposed to have it every four hours, even through the night.

'That time again, I'm afraid,' says the nurse chirpily. 'But I got you a treat for after.'

She holds up a pot of chocolate pudding, which she places on my bedside.

As the oxygen fills my lungs once more, the hissing reminds me of the wolf's words. I need to find the witch and get the hag stone, so I can speak to my parents properly again. Because I know now that the fireflies mean what they say, and if I don't complete their quest my deepest, darkest fear will come true.

CHAPTER 25

A few days in and I'm starting to get bored in the hospital. I've missed one of my Practical Biology lessons so far, which I'm glad about because my mystery seeds – which ended up being pea shoots – are already somehow dead, and we were meant to compare them. I'm a bit annoyed, though, that I've missed a couple of gaming sessions with Omar.

The children's ward is pleasant; rows of beds line each wall, with curtains separating them for privacy. I play board games with the nurses in the mornings after a breakfast of cereal. Next to me is a toddler who keeps leaving me little Lego presents, which I stack on my bedside table. It's now completely full and she's run out of Lego, so I keep secretly putting them back when she's asleep.

Across is a teenage boy who's just had surgery on his leg.

He isn't very talkative and refuses to join in with the board games, but I can see him watch us as we play and I swear he wants to be involved.

I try not to think about the fireflies too much, but with all this free time my mind wanders. I can still feel the wolf's breaths at the back of my neck, hear the thud of the horseman's axe. What will the witch have in store? I imagine, briefly, Grant's storeroom and picture my limbs trapped in a jar.

But then I feel guilty, and I remember how she and Ruby spoke about good witches who helped people. That's what Grant did for me. If I think about it properly, *I'm* the bad one: My parents sent me away and I ruined Grant's home life; I freaked out my friend Ruby and now she isn't speaking to me any more. I keep blaming the fireflies, but what if I'm the problem, what if I'm bad luck? And no matter how many talismans I carry, I'll still bring the consequences of the firefly forest back with me.

The doctor says I'll be home within the week. They're keeping me in to monitor my breathing and continue the course of oxygen through the day and night. The machine is very loud, pumping air into my body in the dark, and it always makes the other children stir. I feel guilty about waking them and wonder whether I'm always going to feel guilty, guilty, guilty about everything.

'You have a visitor,' my favourite nurse, Amanda, tells

me on my third afternoon. It's Monday and I've missed our English lesson. I expect it to be Grant, back from her weekly trip, so I'm surprised when I see Ruby instead.

'Hi,' Ruby says, waving awkwardly from behind Amanda, as if waiting for permission to shuffle forward. I sit up, suddenly feeling very aware that I'm in my *Frozen* PJs, with messed-up hair and a pillow fort surrounding me.

'Oh!' I say. 'Hello.'

Ruby steps forward, a plastic bag clasped in her hands. I glance down, because it seems as if she is presenting me with an offering, though I'm not sure.

'I just wanted to say . . .' Ruby begins, sounding flustered already. 'I'm really, really, *really* sorry for how I reacted the other day.' She looks concerned, her eyes bright. 'I was just surprised, but then I asked my mum about it . . .'

My heart sinks as my worst fear comes true. Everyone will think I'm weird. I want to shrink on to my pillow fort and hide forever.

'No!' says Ruby, reading the feelings on my face. 'No, no, don't worry. It helped. She said that as a good friend I should listen to you, and that everything isn't always what it seems. She even told me off, saying I must have forgotten my Japanese name because that wasn't very compassionate of me.'

A weight that had settled in my chest lifts a little. 'She really said that?'

Ruby nods enthusiastically. 'Mum can be really stern about these things. She even said she understood, but she didn't explain why. She was being very mysterious, actually. Anyway, I brought this to say sorry, and that I'm here for you. Whatever you need. Because . . . Well, I know we haven't been friends long, but I've always struggled with making friends. I don't feel like they understand me, and you make me feel . . . comfortable. So I want to do the same for you.'

It's the most nervous I've ever seen Ruby; her shoulders hunched, eyebrows tight. She sniffs and holds up the bag. I take it from her and peer inside to see a box with a snail shell inside it. I know it's *my* snail shell because I've memorised its pattern. But not only that: she's brought me a ladybird and some frogspawn in a jam jar too.

'I collected all of the lucky things I could find, based on the stuff we researched for our fairy tale. I thought it could . . . help you in the firefly forest.'

I pull the box out and hug it tight. Already I feel safer.

'You know, I don't think a friend would do something like this . . .' I say, glancing up at Ruby with a grin. She looks sad, for a moment, until I finish the last bit of my sentence. '. . . But a *best* friend would.' My cheeks go hot with nerves when I say this. Aside from Omar, who has to like me because he's family, I've never had a best friend.

'Really?' Ruby says, clasping her hands together, jumping

up and down in excitement. She leans in to hug me, and then says, 'Oh, sorry, does that make your breathing worse or –'

I laugh, though it's a little wheezy, which leads to a small coughing fit.

'Don't worry!' I say quickly. 'I'm fine, honestly. Much better. And hugging is fine.'

Ruby looks relieved and perches herself on the end of my bed. She seems deep in thought.

'What is it?' I ask.

She turns to me, her face serious now. 'How was it with the fireflies the other day?'

Something inside me stirs. Hearing mention of the fireflies from someone else's mouth is strange, but freeing too.

'Well . . . they, erm . . .' I feel a little awkward because saying it aloud makes it feel silly, like I'm playing a pretend game. But I'm not. 'The wolf asked me for a hag stone in exchange for the horseshoe. But I'm not sure what that is . . .'

Ruby's eyes light up. 'I do! It's a stone with a naturally formed hole in it. It's said to help you see things for what they truly are.'

Now Ruby starts talking at full speed, connecting the dots between things I hadn't realised before. 'So your quest started with a key . . . And the horseman wants a horseshoe in exchange for it . . . The wolf wants a hag stone . . .

The witch, do you think she might want something?'

'I don't know,' I say. 'I was sort of hoping things would happen in threes, like in fairy tales. But what if it keeps going on and on?'

'Hmm.' Ruby thinks about this for a moment. 'What if you found your *own* hag stone? Like from the beach? Or just bought one online. I've saved up some pocket money . . .'

I shake my head. 'The horseman wanted the horseshoe from the wolf, and the wolf asked for a hag stone from the witch . . .'

'And the fireflies?' says Ruby. 'Did they tell you where to get the key?'

I nod. 'There are specific rules in the firefly forest. A pattern.'

'But the thing is with patterns,' Ruby says. 'You need to see something happen three times before you're sure. So we won't know if things happen in threes until they actually happen.'

'Ugh, you're right,' I say, slumping back. I haven't even told her about the fireflies being afraid of Grant, because then I'll have to mention the jars and it's not my secret to share.

The more we talk, the more confused I get. There's a piece of the puzzle missing, but I don't know what it is yet. And, like Ruby said, the only way to solve it is to carry on doing the quests and hope they end with three, like all the fairy tales we've researched.

'Wait, are you going already?' I ask Ruby as she stands up.

'I'm going to get you some provisions,' she says. 'You had a head torch last time, didn't you?'

I grin. It's so good to have Ruby on board! 'Erm, now that you mention it, that would be great. And maybe some boots too? It can get kind of muddy in the forest . . .'

Ruby nods. 'All right. But when I'm back we actually *do* have quite a bit of schoolwork to catch up with.'

I roll my eyes jokingly. 'Fine,' I say. 'I'll save you an extra chocolate pudding when they come round with food.'

CHAPTER 26

The ants go marching one by one

Hurrah, hurrah

The ants go marching one by one

Hurrah, hurrah

The ants go marching one by one

The little one stops to suck his thumb

And they all march down to the ground

For to get out of the rain

Boom, boom, boom

The song stirs me awake suddenly the next morning. I open my eyes, blearily, and realise the toddler next to me is with her parents and watching a show on a tablet. She claps along with the 'boom boom boom'. Hearing the song again feels like a sign that the fireflies are going to come for me.

Later, Ruby brings me my head torch and wellies, which I hide behind my bed. We check on our talisman box together and study the frogspawn in particular.

'They look like eyes watching us,' I say, glancing at Ruby who seems to find this as interesting as I do.

A flash of the wolf's eyes passes through my mind, but I shake it off.

'Did you know that frogs lay *thousands* of eggs at a time?' Ruby says. 'And the tadpoles aren't actually the eggs, they're what hatch from it.'

'Cool!' I say, before telling Ruby what Grant told me: that a group of frogs is called an army. And even though the thought of seeing the wolf again and meeting the witch scares me, I feel like I can get through it with my best friend's help and my box of luck.

It's just gone midnight when the fireflies appear. I wake to the feeling of something tickling my cheeks and go to scratch at it, then open my eyes when I realise what it is.

'I'm not allowed to leave my bed without letting a nurse know,' I whisper to them, rubbing sleep from my eyes.

The fireflies seem to understand what I'm saying because they crawl beneath my blanket and disappear into the bedspread, one by one. I reach behind me to grab my wellies and head torch, holding firm to my box of luck once I'm secure.

Peering left and right, just to make sure no one's awake, I follow, hoping to return by the time the nurse peeks behind the curtain in two hours for my next round of oxygen.

Crawling through the bedspread is strange. At first, all I can feel is the itchy sheets. But they're quickly replaced by damp grass, and leaves surround my face. My hands land, squelch, in the mud, as I arrive head first.

The forest is foggy tonight, which is why I don't immediately notice the path. Muddy footprints lead through the brambles. Another trail to follow, and I suspect this one will lead me to the witch.

I walk, hands grasped around my box of talismans, until I arrive at the open gate of the witch's house. It looks like Grant's gate – white and neatly lined. Though it's made from marshmallows instead of wood. The house looks a lot like Grant's too, with the door and windows all in the same place, except this one is actually made of gingerbread. There are gingerbread walls oozing with treacle, which I guess is what's holding it together, and windows made of icing.

I only take three steps before I trip, the box rolling away from me, its lid falling open. I see a tree root behind me slithering back into place, and realise it had tripped me. But I thought the trees were on my side, trying to help me?

Now they're only making things more difficult.

I grit my teeth in frustration. What does this forest want from me? It's like a spider's web, pulling me in, wrapping me up in its snare and watching as I slowly lose strength.

I peer into the mud, picking piles of it up, lifting the snail shell and frogspawn back into the box. But I only find two of the three Ruby had collected for me. The ladybird is gone.

A calloused hand covers mine.

I look up, expecting to see a human face, to match. But instead I'm met by the wolf's yellow eyes, shining at me like amber stones, its teeth glinting in the darkness. The hand on mine has turned into a paw.

'You . . . your teeth are so big,' I say, stumbling over my words.

All the better to eat you with, says the wolf, and it lunges.

I scream and fall back as the wolf presses its paws on to my chest. I try to lift it off with both hands but it's too strong. This is what the trees were trying to tell me when they tripped me. They wanted to warn me about the wolf and I didn't listen. And now it's going to gobble me up, and wear my clothes as a disguise for its next victim.

No, it won't, I think. I'm not giving up without a fight, not after everything I've been through. 'If you eat me you won't get your hag stone,' I remind the wolf.

The wolf pushes harder, growling at my words, and it feels for a moment as if all of the air is being squeezed out of my lungs.

Then, relief.

Clever girl, says the wolf, sounding impressed.

It lifts its paw from my chest, and I sit up to catch my breath.

I watch as it gets up and disappears into the fog. Then I rush to the witch's door and knock three times.

Who knocks at my door? the witch asks suspiciously, not opening it to let me in.

'Hazel Al-Otaibi,' I say, feeling for the first time like my name is my own. 'And I'm here to make a request.'

The witch falls silent and I wonder if she's ever going to answer.

It will require payment, she says and my heart sinks. I'd hoped the quest would end here. *Well?* says the witch, when I don't respond.

I hear a shuffle from behind. The wolf is blocking the gate, watching me with hungry eyes. If I deny the witch, the wolf won't get its hag stone, and then it'll have no reason not to attack. But if I agree now, I'll have to carry on the quest for who knows how long. And what if it continues until after Mama and Dad are meant to arrive in England? Will I never see them until I'm done?

'I will bring you payment,' I finally say.

Very well, the witch answers, giving nothing away. *Make your request.*

'A hag stone,' I say quickly and clearly, desperately wanting to get out of the firefly forest. 'I request a hag stone.'

I see, the witch says. *I will give you a hag stone, as you request. In exchange for a white rabbit.*

CHAPTER 27

'Pinch, punch first of the month, no return! White rabbit, white rabbit, white rabbit.'

I'm back at summer school after returning from the hospital. I officially missed out on winning the tree sapling as my pea shoots have died, and I'm behind on my art project, but I'm just about able to keep up with English. I've even managed to bring in Grant's apple pie as my treat for the class. I missed Ezra's last week, but Ruby said they were 'the rockiest rocky roads I've ever tasted in my life', so I don't think I missed out on much.

The doctors say I need to take a brown inhaler twice a day, morning and night. I have a little gadget called a spacer that I breathe through – it lets the medicine circulate so it gets into my lungs. It's kind of fun, in a weird way. And I'm supposed to carry a blue inhaler around and take it whenever I'm struggling to breathe.

Right now, I feel fine, but Ezra's mention of a white rabbit catches my breath.

White rabbit. That's what the witch wants from me.

'Ruby, What does it mean?' I ask my new best friend and walking encyclopaedia. I told her what the next quest was, and right now she looks as confused as I am.

In the end, Ms Basra responds before she can.

'Good question, Hazel,' she says. 'Ezra, would you like to repeat what you just did to Akin?'

Ezra looks horrified. 'I didn't mean it, miss. I was just –'

But Ms Basra laughs. 'I'm asking you to do this because it's relevant to the theme of fairy tales we've been studying.'

'Oh,' says Ezra, looking relieved. I can tell he doesn't like to get in trouble. He repeats what he had done to Akin in front of the rest of us, though this time he mutters 'pinch punch' quickly, seemingly embarrassed.

'Good. Now does anyone know why we do this?' Ms Basra asks.

No one says anything.

'Not even you, Ruby?'

Ruby shakes her head.

'Wow.' Ms Basra laughs. 'I think this is a first. Right, OK, have any of you seen someone throw a pinch of salt over their shoulder?'

'Oh yeah!' Akin answers. 'My mum does that when she cooks.'

'Yes!' says Ms Basra. 'That's exactly what I'm talking about. Has anyone else seen people do that?' Ruby and Ezra nod, but it's not something I've seen before, so Ms Basra explains. 'It's a superstition, to ward off evil spirits. Specifically a witch. The pinch is to weaken her, and the punch is to ward her off for good.'

'But what does the saying mean?' Ruby asks, seemingly frustrated. 'I don't get what any of *that* has to do with a white rabbit.'

'I might have to look that one up!' says Ms Basra, falling silent as she checks her class computer.

We all watch her expectantly.

'Aha, Oh, well, right. So basically there are lots of different theories, but most of them have to do with rabbits being a good luck charm. So you're . . . er, warding away the witch and bringing yourself good luck.'

Ruby turns to me, eyes wide. I know we're thinking about the same thing: my last task.

'NOW then,' Ms Basra says, standing up in front of us once more. She claps her hands together for silence, her watch and bracelet jangling like windchimes. 'Today we're going to focus on subverting a well-known trope in fairy tales.' Ms Basra writes the words 'subvert' and 'trope' on the board and asks us if we know the definitions of the words. This time, Ruby and Akin fight to answer, but I'm finding it hard to concentrate because I keep thinking about the witch in the forest who wants a white rabbit.

Maybe there is a way to stop the tasks for good . . .

But first I need Amélie, Grant's white rabbit for luck.

And, if I'm being truly honest, for bait.

CHAPTER 28

When we arrive back at Grant's house I realise how much it is like a gingerbread house, like Dad said. She's out at the moment, so Ruby and I are on our own. The village is eerily gloomy as we cross the road, clouds blocking the sun, the sound of thunder gradually growing. The storm is edging closer and I wonder if Amélie can sense it.

The fire in the living room is almost completely burned out, and there's a chill inside that seems to follow us wherever we walk.

'So,' Ruby says while I grab us a couple of packets of crisps and squash and sit at the table. 'What are you going to do?'

I sigh. 'I'm going to take Amélie to the firefly forest.'

Ruby gasped. 'You *can't*.'

I purse my lips. 'I *have* to. They'll never leave me alone

otherwise. But I'm not going to let them keep her.' I say the final bit a little more quietly in case the fireflies are around to listen to my deception. I'd never had to worry about them hearing me talk about them before and it makes me feel both comforted to share my thoughts, and more afraid because everything seems far too real now that someone else knows. 'Look, Ms Basra gave me an idea during our lessons.'

By the time I've finished explaining my plan to Ruby, Grant arrives and Ruby's mum follows behind, ready to pick her up.

We linger by the door, in the empty space between the two grown-ups so they don't overhear.

'*Don't* do anything without me,' Ruby says. 'Let's have a weekend sleepover, so I can keep watch when they come.'

I'm about to say that I can't control the fireflies, that it's the other way around. But then maybe I can if I stick close to Grant.

Having Ruby there to back me up would help a lot, especially as I'm really not sure what's going to happen this time now Amélie's involved.

'Ready to go in a bit?' Grant asks, bright and early. I notice the padlock to the secret room is undone, like she's just been inside it. While I sit down at the table she locks it, twisting each number so it's randomised again.

Grant feeds Amélie in her hutch in the kitchen, while I munch my breakfast. Hers is untouched. Grant always feeds Amélie first, says she feels too guilty to eat when Amélie hasn't had anything yet.

I can barely look at Amélie, now that I know the plan, but I try to push it to the back of my mind lest it summons the fireflies.

I hold in a yawn as I sit for breakfast – a glass of orange juice and something called a pikelet, which is like a mini pancake. After Ruby left yesterday afternoon, Grant suggested a day out for the two of us, though she didn't explain what we would be doing, or where we would be going. She just said we would leave after breakfast.

It's the sort of dew-drops-on-grass and foggy-car-window type of early. The world smells fresh after the rain, and the sun is out for the moment. I can see grey clouds in the distance and imagine a battle between the clouds and sun. Perhaps the sun has her own army of fire, and she storms ahead, blowing the clouds away. Meanwhile, the clouds gather, wait, reserve their energy, until they're ready for another rush of thunder.

I like seeing how the weather changes in England. Back home it's predictable: sunny, always sunny. No clouds to turn into shapes, no rain to smell, no cold to breathe in. I watch the clouds above the trees as we drive, and see a butterfly flit across the sky. It reminds me of the caterpillar in its cocoon in Grant's garden. Is it a butterfly now? Flying free, fully transformed?

Grant doesn't speak, and neither do I, but it doesn't feel uncomfortable. She plays old, crackly music from her radio with lots of trumpets. I can feel the road beneath me, each bump sending me up into the air.

We pass by the hospital, which is on the outer edges of the nearby town, and slalom our way through the streets. The town here looks old too: cobbled pavements and yellow-stained buildings that look as if they've been there for hundreds of years. Then, occasionally, a tall high-rise that reminds me of the buildings in Kuwait. I turn my attention to the small groups of people trickling out on to the road.

The further in we get, the more the quiet fades into a crescendo of noise.

The world is alive and humming by the time Grant pulls up in front of an old building, held up with yellowing pillars and intricately carved roses.

There's a sign that reads: 'Little Nook Mental Health Centre'.

'What's this?' I ask, which sounds silly, because the sign explains. But I guess I mean *Why are we here?*

'I thought,' Grant begins, and I can hear she sounds a little nervous for some reason. 'That I'd tell you where I go every Monday. And explain exactly what it is in those little jars in my secret room . . .'

CHAPTER 29

'It started many, many, many . . .' Grant laughs at herself, 'years ago, when I was just a little bit younger than you. I started to worry about things I had never worried about before: about my parents getting ill, if friends were annoyed with me, if I was doing badly at school. The worries grew and grew each day until they consumed me.

'One morning, I was walking to school on a chilly day just after Christmas, when I noticed, trailing behind me, a strange creature. It was the most frightening thing I'd ever seen, a bouncing head, with grey eyes, watching me, hopping along to match each of my steps. I tried to move away from it quickly, but it snapped at my ankles with fangs instead of teeth, and it snuffed and snorted all the way.

'By the time I arrived at school my heart was pounding and I was too scared to go into lessons with the creature following me. No matter what I tried, it kept coming back, and I stopped being able to concentrate in lessons and avoided all of the places I'd last seen the creature. Soon the only place that felt safe was home, until one day I stepped out of my bedroom to see it watching me, with its pale grey eyes and sallow stretched skin.'

'That's awful,' I whisper, the hairs on the back of my neck standing on end. It's like being back in the firefly forest, with an impossible task ahead.

'The monster followed me around for years,' Grant continues. 'And occasionally it brought with it others. It was only when I was much older, living on my own, that I decided to seek help. I came here . . .' Grant nods at the sign we'd pulled up to, 'and spoke to someone. And you know what they did?'

I shake my head, watching Grant in wonder.

'They told me what the creatures were. Demons. My inner demons spawned from my worries. And they helped me fight them – not with weapons, but with kind words to myself, with the help of those who care about me, and with a strength I didn't know I had inside.'

Grant takes a deep breath, and I find myself mimicking her. The heater is on, the windows in the car fogged, and my mind is whirring.

'I began to understand who those demons were, what they wanted. So now I talk to someone who can help me fight them. Then I drive to the garden centre and buy a new jar to keep my demons locked inside. That's what's hidden in that room.'

It takes me a few moments to realise Grant has ended her story, but my mind is bursting with questions. 'Why do they look like . . . Well, like brains and guts and scary things?'

Grant wrinkles her nose. 'I know they look a bit odd. But in reality they start as a seed, and grow in the jars into the shapes of my worries. They're no more strange than the roots of the flowers I grow in my garden.'

My next question follows on quickly. 'Why do you keep them?'

Grant sighs at this. 'I suppose, I haven't been ready to let them go. Not yet, anyway. Even though I'm much older than you and lucky enough to have help, I still have a way to go, I think.'

I chew my lip for a bit, thinking about her words. Grant's demons remind me of the fireflies. When I turn to her I see her eyes soften and I think, maybe she knows. I think she's trying to help me.

'We all have our demons,' Grant says. 'They come in different shapes and sizes, and I just want to say that if *you* ever need to speak about them, I'm here.'

I'm not quite ready to speak to Grant about the fireflies yet. Having Amélie involved makes it harder to explain everything. But I think I finally understand now why the fireflies are afraid of Grant: because she has the tools, the proper tools to make them go away. I think, though, I can ask her a question that doesn't give too much away.

'When you were, or are . . . fighting your demons,' I ask. 'Did you ever want to give up?'

Grant laughs. 'All the time! It's like having a cold – it gets worse before it gets better and sometimes you want to give in to it. But I promise that at the end of that scary path is a ray of sunshine.'

Grant's response to my question is spookily accurate, like she can read my mind, and I decide I've asked enough for now.

When we're done we go to a garden centre for morning cake and tea.

'I always thought you did everything on your own,' I say to Grant, after a bit.

Grant laughs at this, almost a cackle. 'Oh no, oh no, oh no. I might not be like your parents: married with a child, but that doesn't mean there are people I haven't loved in my life, in the same way they love each other.'

I ask Grant about the photos of her with that woman. The ones in her house. Her face softens when I mention her.

'We travelled the world together,' Grant says. 'Fifty countries . . . It was wonderful. And can you imagine me planning to do that?'

'Not really,' I admit, thinking of Grant's schedule.

'I've lived through lots of different chapters in my life. What you see here isn't the whole of it. Not even close. But your story is just beginning. And with that I have one more surprise. Follow me!'

Grant grabs my hand in hers and we wander up and down the aisles of the garden centre until we arrive at shelves stacked with different-shaped jars.

'Which one would you like?' she asks.

I peer at one that is round like a fishbowl. It has a yellow polka-dot lid. 'This one. But what's it for?'

'*Your* demons,' Grant says, handing it to me like it's a crown and I'm about to be made a queen.

And I realise, with her and Ruby's help, that I'm finally ready to face the fireflies again.

CHAPTER 30

When Ruby comes over later, it's time.

We spend the evening watching TV while Grant works at her desk. When she goes up to her room at nine she reminds us to 'turn the lights off before you go to bed', and says that a special end-of-summer-holidays breakfast will be ready in the morning. Then she leaves us in silence, while we wait.

Ruby and I don't say a thing as Amélie shuffles across the room. She's acting skittish again, and moments later I hear the telltale sign of thunder. Ruby and I rush over to the window and see lightning too. The storm has finally arrived.

'Are you *sure* about this?' Ruby asks. 'I know you think you need to take her, but what if your plan goes wrong?'

I've never seen her so uncertain, so unsure, and I realise

that perhaps this is the one thing I know just a little bit more about.

I lead her across the room to sit down on the sofas again. Amélie jumps up between us, cowering in my lap. 'I've told you a bit about the fireflies,' I say. 'But there's more.' I tell her about their visits in Kuwait, and that I *know* my plan will work, because I know them better than I know myself.

'I feel like I'm never alone,' I explain. 'But not in a good way. It's like there's always someone watching me, judging me. I don't know when they'll appear – sometimes it's sudden. Other times I can feel it build up, like a storm, but I don't have the power to stop it. They make me feel angry, scared and helpless, all at the same time. And no matter what I do to ignore them, I can't seem to get rid of them for good. And so I'm doing the only thing I know how to: end this horrible quest and stop my deepest, darkest fear from coming true. I know they won't go away forever – they'll be back. But sometimes their quests aren't as bad. This one is the worst I've had.'

As I admit the truth of it, the words tumbling out of my mouth at speed, I feel relieved. It helps to talk to someone about it properly, and I'm not sure I could have said all of this without Grant's chat earlier. Finding out she *isn't* doing everything alone after all, and talking about it to someone, has helped me realise that maybe I can do the same.

Still, it's one thing to tell Ruby about the fireflies and their quest, and another thing to tell her how it makes me feel. But as she peers back at me, her eyes watery with unshed tears, I know she understands.

Ruby nods a few times, and then she asks, 'What will make you feel better again?'

This takes me aback. I've spent so much time thinking about what will stop the fireflies from making everything worse that I haven't begun to imagine feeling different. Feeling better. Being asked, I realise I don't know.

'Don't worry,' Ruby says after seeing my expression. 'I'm on it.'

She marches as quietly as an ant across the room and pulls open the cupboards, one by one, scanning each thoroughly.

'Salt!' Ruby declares, pulling out an almost-full jar of cooking salt. She shakes it, just to be sure. 'That should be enough.'

'How do you know?' I ask. 'Have you ever repelled a witch before?'

Ruby rolls her eyes, clearly unimpressed by my lack of faith in her. 'It'll be enough.'

I nod, feeling better. 'OK,' I say. 'What else?'

'Erm,' says Ruby, shuffling around. 'I don't know . . . Just, don't . . . walk under a ladder or break a mirror?'

'What?' I ask.

Ruby scrunches up her nose. 'Just some superstitions. Seven years of bad luck if you break a mirror . . .'

The room is a fizz of excitement now, and with Ruby's help I feel as ready as I can be. I have my head torch on, salt in my left pocket, my plan at the fore of my mind. And I have a friend. Now all I need is Amélie.

'Where's she gone?' shrieks Ruby, forgetting to be quiet. She looks inside cupboards and underneath tables. She's getting a little overexcited. So am I. We're both slowly becoming hysterical, like all of my anxieties are a great big glass of fizzy drink, ready to spill over.

'Probably hiding,' I say, suppressing a nervous giggle. 'From all this noise.'

'Ooops, sorry,' says Ruby sheepishly.

We search quietly this time, creeping round the living room like thieves in the night; we search in the bathroom and in the attic room that will one day soon be Mama and Dad's. Grant's room is shut, of course, because she's sound asleep. Eventually, we find Amélie hiding beneath my bed and I try to ignore the guilt that she's got involved in all of this.

'One more thing,' I say, rushing to my bedside table. I pack my blue inhaler – the one I'm supposed to use for emergencies – along with my lucky charms, and only then do I feel fully armoured for my quest ahead.

I crawl beneath the bed to reach Amélie, to get ready

to do what we need to do. Her whole body is shaking, her whiskers twitching, her eyes darting around frantically.

I pull Amélie's body, preparing to stroke her and calm her down with a treat, but something else pulls back.

At the back of my bed, on the wall behind the headboard, is a concrete hole, with leaves slithering out of it, reaching. There are a pair of eyes staring out at me, and for a moment I think it's the witch, coming to claim her prize, until I recognise the fireflies.

The fireflies don't need to scratch and pull at my skin this time, because their magic is pulling Amélie instead. Dragging her.

Amélie squeals in fright as she's pulled into the darkness, the sounds she makes ripping into my heart.

'I have to go now,' I say to Ruby from underneath the bed, my voice shaking.

Ruby bends down and peers at me, looking as scared as I feel.

I slip into the dark, dark hole, the vines wrapping around my body, helping me through.

And I follow Amélie, hoping against hope that my plan works and we both get safely back home.

CHAPTER 31

I can't see Amélie when I enter the forest and immediately I panic. She's not protected from the wolf or the horseman, or whatever else rustles in the dark. And if the witch gets hold of her before I have the chance to carry out my plan . . . Ruby said it was rabbits' feet that were lucky, and I don't want to find out what that means for Amélie.

It's different knowing someone else might be hurt by the fireflies' tricks. When it's me, I can swallow it down, face it. Just about. And, anyway, I'm sort of used to it now. But when it's another living, breathing creature, one that relies on me to keep it safe . . . that's different.

The firefly forest is eerily quiet today, almost too quiet, like it's holding its breath, waiting for something.

I'm in a different part of the forest this time, so I don't recognise my bearings, or how to get to the witch's cottage from here. I crouch down, searching for footprints, or breadcrumbs, like Hansel and Gretel, but all I see are ants as large as a rabbit. And the song floats into my head:

The ants go marching one by one
Hurrah, hurrah
The ants go marching one by one
Hurrah, hurrah
The ants go marching one by one
The little one stops to suck his thumb
And they all march down to the ground
For to get out of the rain
Boom, boom, boom.

I follow them, like I used to in Kuwait, knowing deep down that they're leading me where I need to go. All round the forest ground, dotted throughout after the rain, are a troop of tall mushrooms, some springing up to my shoulders. I don't know what mushrooms mean, whether they're good luck or bad, but I hope they'll help me find Amélie.

Eventually, the ants disappear, but the mushrooms continue, growing more spores now, one at the base of each tree. They seem kind of like checkpoints, so I follow, until I start to become familiar with my surroundings.

Soon I discover I'm on a path that is a replica of my walk

home from school. I peer to the left, where the paddock and Shetland pony should stand, only to find a broken-down fence eaten up by gorse.

Up close, I can see the nicks in the tree bark, like open wounds, blood pouring out of them, trickling to the forest floor. The mushrooms are gone now and it's just a trail of blood that stops suddenly in the middle of my path. But then I see them, bloodied paw prints in the mud, hop, hop, hopping between closely growing trees. And I step off the path to follow.

I know these prints belong to Amélie, but I don't know whether it's just the blood of the trees or her blood too that is mixing with it, and I start to pick up pace until I'm running. It's humid, a different sort of heat to the dry air in Kuwait, and I start to sweat almost at once.

Then I find it, the white marshmallow gate, the paw prints stopping at the steps to the front door. As I reach for the gate latch, it snaps. The fence melts away in the rain, leaving a puddle of goo behind.

I suddenly feel hungry, so hungry. The steps up to the front door are made from biscuits, and I pull a slab apart, dipping it into the icing to eat.

Each bite makes me hungrier, and I want to eat and ask the witch for more. The flowers taste like sugar sweets, the fallen leaves, crisps. Chocolate mud crumbles like cake, and soon my hands are coated and sticky . . .

And that's when I realise I'm being tricked, somehow, lured to eat and eat forever, the way the fireflies scratch and scratch. But I have more important things to do: save Amélie, collect the hag stone, horseshoe and key, and STOP this quest for good.

I take my shoes off now, so I can walk silently, and creep along the wet grass in my socks, feeling the water seep through, cooling me. Stepping on to the biscuit floor of the porch, I can hear the witch humming a tune from the kitchen. It's the one about the ants marching, the one I was singing just moments before.

As I step into the kitchen, the spell that had taken over outside lifts. Amélie cowers in a cage made from spun sugar. In the corner, a pot of stock and herbs boils, and the witch lines up a set of knives and other unfamiliar sharp objects on the table. She starts sharpening one of them, and the clashing sound of metal on metal sets my teeth on edge.

All along the ceiling are hanging objects: four-leaf clovers, light-catchers, which throw rainbows, and evil eyes. All symbols of luck. There's one empty hook that looks just the right size for a rabbit's foot and I know I have to act now, before it's too late.

I slip into the room as silently as I can, pulling the pack of salt from my pouch and pouring it in a circle around Amélie. I do this so quickly the witch only turns as I'm stuffing the salt back into my bag.

She looks between me and Amélie, drops the knife she was sharpening on to the counter, and then she laughs and laughs and laughs.

CHAPTER 32

I don't expect this reaction, and so the speech I had planned trickles out of my mouth in stops and starts. I'm distracted by other things too, like the fact that the witch looks familiar. An older version of me.

'You have to follow the rules . . . er . . . don't you?' I say, not meaning it to end in a question. The fireflies' rules – knocking on wood, not letting me leave until I'd completed a task – made me realise that there is something unspoken in this place. 'I gave you the rabbit as you requested.' My voice grows in confidence as I think of Ruby standing at the front of our summer school lessons, explaining certain rules and tropes of fairy tales. 'But you didn't specify what for, did you? And . . . and so here it is, but you can't touch it because of the salt. And you can't keep it.'

The witch's eyes – my eyes – are gleaming, almost as if she's proud. I might not be able to get my words out quite as well as Ruby does, but my thoughts are still there, and they're worth expressing.

The witch walks up to me slowly, the knife back in her hand, and I hold the salt out, in case I need to protect myself, and get ready to complete the enchantment with a punch. But she stops short, holds her right hand out, palms up.

On it is what I think is an ordinary rock, until I see a big gaping hole through it.

The hag stone.

My stomach churns. *It worked.*

This is finally it. The end of my quest. I just need to give the hag stone to the wolf in exchange for the horseshoe, and give the horseshoe to the horseman in exchange for the key. Once I give the key to the fireflies I'm certain they'll release me this time. Then Amélie will be OK, my deepest, darkest fear won't come true, and whatever comes next: I'll be prepared. Because I'm not alone. I have Ruby and Grant.

I turn to Amélie, she looks petrified in her corner, but leaving her within the protection of the salt ring is her best chance at staying safe.

'I'll be back,' I say. 'I promise.'

I take the hag stone and the witch just stands there, watching me.

Well, go on, she says, a lingering smile on her face. *Look through it.*

I raise it to my eye, not knowing what to expect. And I gasp when I see that through the hag stone the witch isn't standing there at all. Instead, there's just a single firefly, dancing across the room. Removing the hag stone, I see the witch again, and her shining eyes remind me of the fireflies' bodies.

It was them all along. The fireflies are the witch, the wolf and the horseman.

Thunder strikes, and Amélie lets out a squeak. I feel awful leaving her there, but I'm so close to completing the quest. I just need to find the wolf and horseman and then I will return for her.

I leave in a rush, feeling excited now instead of scared. But as I cross the forest again, something doesn't feel right. It feels all wrong, wrong, wrong. But I don't have time to think about it, because I need to get to the wolf.

It starts to rain, just a drizzle, and the trees help me through the forest, guiding me to the wolf's cave. They sway left and right in a dance. Looking closely I can see their branches point me to where I need to go. The wind is wailing, or is it the trees? It's hard to tell now as everything blends into one.

I stop for a moment and pull the hag stone from my pocket again. Once I give it to the wolf, I won't get the chance to see this place for what it really is. And so I look through it now and inspect my surroundings.

The firefly forest I see through the hag stone is different. It's nothing like the one in Snow White, or the one Ruby spoke about in our second lesson. Instead, the trees are my defences, the blood coming out of them is the shadows of my mind, gushing: the guilt, the worries, the anxiety, all bundled into one. It's why they're wailing. It's why they've helped me all this time. And as my quest grew bigger and scarier, they grew with it, showing me that even though I don't always know it, I have the strength inside me to fight the fireflies. Here, everything I feel seeps out freely, but maybe that's what I need to do in the real world to stop them coming back.

I spend the rest of the route peering through the hag stone, and it's like looking inside my own mind to find the questions and worries I had buried deep, now seeping from the blood in the trees:

Did Dad send me away the same way his parents did? *No.*

Does Grant regret me staying with her, after all the trouble I put her through? *No.*

Is Ruby just friends with me because she feels sorry for me? *No.*

All of these thoughts spilling on to the forest floor, and the wails turn to whispers once more.

The hag stone. The hag stone. The hag stone, they remind me.

I think of Amélie at the witch's house, and Ruby in my room, waiting for me, and I start to run, my footsteps drumming against the beating heart of the forest floor.

CHAPTER 33

When I see the snail's shell, like a beacon of light in the distance, I know I'm close. The snail – it's here for me again, to protect me from the wolf and its hunger.

I watch through the hag stone as the firefly comes out of its cave and glides over to me, landing on a rock just in front of me. When I pull the hag stone from my eye I see the wolf, its eyes shining, mouth dripping with saliva. Each step it takes towards me makes the ground rumble.

But it stops a distance from the snail.

I see you visited the witch, it says, with a voice that comes from nowhere. A voice that hisses like the fireflies' whispers, *You'll understand, I'm sure, why she has so many protections at her door.*

I don't understand what the wolf means, for a moment, but then I remember another story I'd come across from a fairy tale. Little Red Riding Hood. About the old woman who lives in a cottage in the woods alone, and a wolf who swallows her whole. And then I remember that fireflies eat each other, and I don't quite know what it all means, except this place is full of rules that feel like chaos, and I find myself so tangled up in them that I don't know how to make my way back out again.

It's like being caught in a spider's web, too full of its stickiness to free myself.

'What about the horseman, then?' I ask. 'Why don't you try to eat him?'

The wolf laughs, a wheezy laugh, just like the witch did. It worries me. I'm always a step behind, always missing a piece of information.

The horseman would have my head, says the wolf. *Why do you think I live here? In the marsh? His horse is too scared to cross, lest it sink into the mud. You think because we come and collect you together, that we are one ourselves. But it shows you have so much more to learn about this place.*

I don't know if the wolf's words are a hint, or a warning, but I don't want to speak to him longer than I need to. Just being around him, the smell of death that lingers on his fur makes my throat prickle.

I step forward three paces, closing the gap between us. The snail is behind me in case I need it, but right now

I don't feel like I do. One hand is wrapped around my blue inhaler, the other holding out the hag stone.

The wolf crouches, like he's ready to leap for me. His nose is the size of my palm, and his mouth is as long as my arm. For a moment, I think I've made a horrible mistake, but then I realise he's bowing, intending me to place the hag stone on his head.

Once I have, he removes a paw from the muddy ground to reveal a brass horseshoe. And without another word, he walks away.

I feel relieved and stunned that he hasn't put up a fight, but that in itself is suspicious to me.

Why? I wonder. *What does he gain from letting me get away alive now he has the hag stone?*

This is more than just following rules. The fireflies need me – I'm what sustains them, feeds their desires. As I leave the wolf's domain, the horseshoe in my clutches, I'm not as confident about my mission any more.

The firefly forest has turned silent as I stand there, planning my next steps. I visited the witch's house first, then the wolf's. But I realise now I don't know where the horseman lives – I've only ever seen him in the woods.

I rack my brains, trying to think where he would be. And then I remember what Ruby said about the Black Forest

– a horseman living in an underwater lair. But where, in this forest, could there be a lake?

Think, Hazel, think!

But I'm used to Ruby helping me with this bit – puzzling pieces together that don't make sense. I can't return to her now, though, because the firefly forest won't spit me out until I've finished the tasks. I should have asked for help sooner, should have told Grant about the fireflies when she told me about the jars. Maybe she could've figured out how to scare them away.

I sink to the floor and the tree branches cradle me, holding me up like a baby in its cot. I do what I did on the very first night here in England: I rewind my life backwards, will it all not to have happened.

I rewind summer school, return to a time before I was friends with Ruby. But I realise the idea of that makes me sad, and I think I'd rather live through the bad moments for the good ones.

I rewind stealing the apple and letting Amélie get a hold of it: the single act that got me into trouble.

As I'm about to rewind the journey back to the airport, my brain pauses the memory. When I first arrived at Grant's house in the dark, all I could hear was the trickling of water. At the back of her garden is a little pond. And here in the forest, the witch's house looks oddly familiar.

Perhaps, just perhaps, the pond is where the horseman lives. And like everything else here, it's bigger.

I run again, retracing the trail of mushrooms that had led me to the witch's cottage. Thunder and lightning follow me, clapping and zapping at each step I take.

This time, I sneak round the side of the witch's house, and deep into her garden. It's bigger than Grant's. Wilder. The flowers reach out for me, but not as if they want to help. It's like they want to eat me whole, consume my flesh and bones and use them for fuel to grow bigger. They have teeth instead of buds, and nails instead of thorns. They're beautiful and deadly all at once, their scent inviting me to lean forward . . .

But now I can hear it, the rush of water. And where Grant's pond sits in her garden, here in the firefly forest is a great lake, completely clear. Deep underwater I see a buried castle, a maze of brick tunnels leading to the centre of it. There are four turrets at each corner and a drawbridge at its entrance. That must be where the horseman lives, but I'm not sure how I'll be able to get down there.

I've never been a very good swimmer, but I just need to reach the entrance of the tunnel, don't I? Swim straight down. But then, how do I breathe?

I'm half distracted, which is why I don't notice the shadow approach at first. I turn around and realise, too late, that it's a giant frog, mouth open wide, croaking the way my belly does when it's hungry.

Darkness engulfs me as the frog gobbles me up and swallows me whole.

CHAPTER 34

Inside the frog's belly it's dark and sticky.

I expect it to start chewing, though I'm not sure if frogs have teeth or not. But instead I feel a rumble and a splash, and it's as if I've been stuck in a tumble dryer spinning round and round and round.

I went on a roller coaster once, and it was a bit like this. Each movement made my belly swoop and loop and I counted every second, waiting for it to end. But just like the ride, the frog halts suddenly, and I wait, covered in goo wondering what'll happen next.

The frog croaks, reverberating in my head like I'm in the middle of a ringing bell. I'm starting to feel hot and sick and want this all to be over.

But then, the frog opens its mouth and spits me back out.

I land on a cold damp floor and open my eyes to see

I'm inside a dark tunnel, its walls dripping with water. There are fire lanterns dotted along each side of the brick structure, reminding me of an old, medieval castle. A small window stands to my right, and I peer out of it to find the forest is gone.

I'm underwater, in the castle I saw from the lake's surface, and there are shrubs and plants swaying, water floating past making everything a haze. The drip, drip, dripping is coming from small cracks on the wall, and every once in a while the structure groans. The sound sends shivers down my spine as I imagine what would happen if it collapsed.

The sound of a croak draws my attention back to the frog. It sits silently, watching me. I know instinctively that it's a friend, not a foe. And I wonder if, like the snail, this frog has grown from one of the frogspawn I left behind. Maybe that's another reason the tree tripped me – so I'd leave it here to grow and help me.

The frog doesn't speak to me, not like the wolf does, but I believe it'll be waiting for my return.

There are other windows at intervals all along the tunnel, and through them I can see the bottom of the lake. I walk down the maze of tunnels, getting lost at each turn, all the while the water drip, drip, drips in a steady rhythm.

There's nothing to lead me, nothing to show me the way like in the forest – no blood, no mushrooms, no footsteps. It's eerily quiet, aside from the structure groaning, and

I find myself worried that I'll never make it to the horseman or back to the frog. What if I'm stuck here forever, roaming tunnel after tunnel for eternity? My parents will arrive in England and wonder where I am. Or maybe they won't and that's the point of losing the quest . . . Ruby will forget about me and move on to secondary school; Grant will wait, because deep down I think she'd know, and blame herself.

No, I think, gritting my teeth. *I'm so close.*

And there's Amélie of course, still trapped. Frightened.

I sing my old song, the one I go to for comfort:

> *The ants go marching one by one*
> *Hurrah, hurrah*
> *The ants go marching one by one*
> *Hurrah, hurrah*
> *The ants go marching one by one*
> *The little one stops to suck his thumb*
> *And they all march down to the ground*
> *For to get out of the rain*
> *Boom, boom, boom*

That's when I notice the drips are dripping in rhythm with the beat of the song. They're showing me the way. I stop at a crossroads and listen to each tunnel in turn, all the while whispering the song.

The ants go marching one by one
Hurrah, hurrah
Left.
The ants go marching one by one
Hurrah, hurrah
Right.
The ants go marching one by one
The little one stops to suck his thumb
Straight ahead.
And they all march down to the ground
For to get out of the rain
Boom, boom, boom

I stop in front of a great big door. I reach for the handle, but it opens without me needing to push, and there he stands at the centre of the room on his horse. Except he's just a stone statue, made from the same material as the walls.

I walk closer, aware of my echoing footsteps, until I'm right in front of them both. Neither move, but the horse has its front foot poised, as if waiting for its shoe. I pull it out of my pocket and put into place.

A moment of silence, stillness. Then the horse rears, flesh and bone again, and I worry it will land on my chest and send me flying across the room. I dodge it, so instead the horse lands hard on the floor, its hooves echoing louder than my footsteps, forcing me to hold my hands up against my ears.

Another sound challenges the horse's. A great groan. A piece of rock smashes to the floor, missing the horse by centimetres. It whinnies in surprise, but the horseman says nothing, does nothing. I see him grip firm as he leads his horse out of the tunnel, just as a jet of water lands, flooding the room at once.

In the place where the horse had stood is a key. The skeleton key. I pick it up and stuff it in my pocket so it sits next to my inhaler.

Get out, I tell myself.

The castle walls are collapsing with the force of the horse's hooves, and the lake is flooding into it. I need to leave. Now.

I wade through the water, trying to go quickly, but the force of it slows me down. I try to hop across like a frog, but I don't have the right limbs. Eventually, I get out of the room and into the tunnels and find myself having to swim through them. I'm a little bit quicker, but still too slow. The horseman and his horse are gone. It's just me.

Walls crumble around me as I swim, swim, swim.

I take my last breath, just as the tunnel fills up completely, and dive beneath the water, trying to remember the path back.

Then I see the frog swimming towards me, mouth open wide. And I swim right inside it.

Back on the shore I cough and splutter. Water has gone down my throat, up my nose and into my ears. I sneeze violently, and by the time I open my eyes, the frog is gone. Instead, floating above me are the three fireflies.

The horseman made it out, I see. And I don't know why but part of me feels sad. I had hoped they would disappear now, leave me alone, but instead I hear their familiar hissing as they speak.

Well done. Well done. Well done, they praise.

You retrieved the key.

I breathe a sigh of relief, waiting for them to release me, to tell me this is all over, but they don't. Instead they say:

With this key, find the sleeping dragon's lair and unlock its chest of treasures.

It hits me that my quest hasn't ended at all. It's only just begun.

I don't respond.

The fireflies speak again:

We thought you enjoyed stealing, they say, and I sense a danger in their words. *Apples are only the beginning. With this key you can steal lots of things . . . and bring them to us in exchange for a rew—*

'No!' I finally say, interrupting them. 'No! No! No!'

You remember what happens when you defy us? the fireflies say. *We won't let you leave. Not until you agree. And if you don't do as we say, your deepest, darkest fear will come true: your parents will leave you here alone with Grant.*

Hearing my worst fear spoken aloud again sends a jolt of panic through me. But instead of letting it eat me up, the way fireflies gobble each other, instead of letting it defeat me, I turn that panic into determination.

All of these rules, all of them, I follow them carefully and everything still goes wrong. It makes no sense.

Because maybe it's not about following rules, a voice says. Not the fireflies this time. Me. *Maybe it's about breaking them.*

I don't have to listen to the fireflies, follow their instructions. By refusing to give them what they want, I can finally take control of my story. No matter the consequences. Because even though I'm more scared than I've ever been right now, I need to face my fears, not hide from them.

In front of me is the door of the witch's house with Amélie inside it. I wrap my fingers around the key and grip it firm.

CHAPTER 35

My feet stomp, stomp, stomp towards the open door of the witch's house. It's only when I'm safely across the threshold that I turn to look outside. I expect to see the fireflies chasing me – either in that form, or as the witch, the headless horseman and the wolf – but the smell of smoke alerts me to what I'm about to see.

The rain has stopped and everything is suddenly dry in the forest. The fireflies are gone. In their wake is a trail of fire, slowly licking the roots of the trees, crawling upwards. The trees screech, and the sound of it reverberates through my teeth and bones like the pain is inside me.

My defences. The fireflies are burning them down, trying to teach me a lesson. I watch, for a moment, as the trees burn, the fire inching closer and closer to the witch's house.

All the feelings I try to bury deep inside me are gushing

out like the red sap pouring from the trees. I'm scared and frustrated and angry. Sometimes it all feels hopeless, like now. But Grant said she felt that way too, didn't she? And that, like a cold, it gets worse before it gets better. She kept pushing, kept fighting. So I have to do the same. Starting with Amélie.

She's in the witch's house, sitting there cowering in the corner in her spun-sugar cage. I break it open and I hold her in my arms and rock her like a baby as the fire burns and the trees scream. We're trapped, the flames circling us, licking at the windows like a hungry animal. The smell of burnt cake lingers in the air, so sickly it makes me cough. I'm struggling to breathe, and take my blue inhaler twice, like the doctors instructed, for relief.

I don't know how long I sit there, curled up with Amélie in my arms, while the forest around me dies. Maybe it'll melt away entirely, the way it does when I complete parts of the quest, and I'll wake up back home. Or maybe we'll be stuck here forever, like the fireflies warned. Even though the fireflies aren't scratching at me now, I still feel them drawing me to them.

Then their voices appear once more, threefold, cutting like ice through the burning heat:

It's not too late. It's not too late. It's not too late.

Release the rabbit and we'll let you go home. You'll see your parents, and when you return, your next quest will begin.

'And what then? What about Grant? How will she feel to lose Amélie?'

The fireflies don't respond. I don't expect them to. None of that concerns them. The only thing that exists in their world is their need to feed.

One more chance. One more chance. One more chance. Will you accept? Will you accept? Will you accept? they eventually say. But their words only make me tighten my grip on Amélie's soft fur, her quivering body seeking solace in my arms. Maybe the fireflies are right, and if I don't listen to them now my parents will leave me the way Dad's did. And maybe I'll be stuck in this burning forest forever. But I can't fulfil their quests any longer. They've asked for too much.

'No,' I say with my last breath, as my throat chokes up. But it's not my asthma this time. It's panic, melting my determination. I feel so lost and alone and I don't know what to do. I start to make promises to myself and the people I love, a bargain between us if I get out of here:

I'll tell my parents the truth about the fireflies.

I'll be the best friend to Ruby, and help her as much as she's helped me.

I'll help Grant release her demons.

Soon after, a ladybird lands on my knee, and a new song, like the one I used to sing about the ants, but a rhyme instead, worms its way into my mind.

> *Ladybird, ladybird, fly away home,*
> *Your house is on fire, your children are gone.*

Grant said that you should make a wish on a ladybird that lands on you. So I wish she would take her with me, away from this place, and Amélie too, back to where we belong.

> *Ladybird, ladybird, fly away home,*
> *Your house is on fire, your children are gone.*

I sing out loud now, coughing from the smoke. And the ladybird leaves my knee and flies up the stairs of the witch's cottage and through a hole in the wall that looks like a crumbling biscuit nibbled by sharp, fang-like teeth.

> *Ladybird, ladybird, fly away home,*
> *Your house is on fire, your children are gone.*

Finally, the ladybird flies though. And like I followed the ants, and the fireflies, I follow her now, hoping the luck she brings me will take me home.

CHAPTER 36

When I crawl out from under the bed once more it's almost sunrise. Ruby is snoozing on the floor where I left her hours before. She opens her eyes slightly as Amélie brushes past her in a blur, scratching at my bedroom door to be let out. And when Ruby sees me follow, pulling myself up from under my bed, she bundles me into the warmest hug I've ever been given, her hair a blanket wrapping around me, safe.

'I'm so glad you're alive,' she says, her voice croaky like the frog's. 'So I can kill you myself. NEVER do that again.'

We laugh about it for a while, even though we both know I can't keep that promise. We don't talk about the firefly forest, not yet. Instead we both curl up like cats on my bed, sleeping as much as we can before Grant calls us down for our breakfast feast, which turns out to be eggy bread with fruit and syrup and cream. Ruby leaves soon after, promising to return in the afternoon to finish our project. We just need the ending to our story, which I have now. The one I lived through. And this time, I can't wait to share it with her.

When we're alone I clear the table, while Grant packs up our leftovers and feeds Amélie.

'Great-Aunt Hazel,' I say, calling her that in full for the first time.

She turns to me slowly, her eyes focused. 'Yes, Great-Niece Hazel?' she replies, and I grin.

'Remember when you told me about your jars? And . . . the place you visit and your demons?'

Grant stops what she's doing, returns to the table, and gives me her full attention. 'Yes, I do.'

I nod, still clearing up, because I'm struggling to say what I need to while also looking her in the eye. 'Well . . . there are these fireflies . . .' I begin, and she doesn't look surprised.

'Have they visited again?' she asks, her voice soft, soothing.

Something about her question, the fact that she already knows makes me burst into tears. As Grant rushes over to me, and rubs my back, everything I've gone through over the last few weeks comes gushing out of my mouth.

'B-but I didn't listen to them, this time,' I finish.

And I tell her how our chat helped, and how I think maybe I can stop following them.

All the while Grant nods.

When I'm finished speaking and crying, I feel tired. But there's one more thing I need to do. Something that'll help both me and Grant, I think.

'Can I see your demons properly?'

My question surprises her, but she walks over to the door, unlocking it and pulling it open. She stands aside and I look past. In the morning light her demons look less scary, and it's kind of like that with the fireflies. They are more like misshapen vegetables with roots poking out.

'I think we should bury them in the garden,' I say. 'Not so they can grow,' I add. 'But so that you can say goodbye to them, like I did the fireflies.'

It's Grant's turn for tears now, and she pulls me in for a fierce hug. Where Ruby's was like a warm mug of hot chocolate, Grant's is sharp, like her apple pie. 'I think you're right,' she finally says.

Before we go into the garden I remember to take two pumps of my brown asthma inhaler, like I did last night, and pocket my blue one, just in case. We pass by the flower that held the caterpillar's cocoon, to see it empty, the butterfly long gone.

'How about here?' Grant suggests, finding a bare patch of grass by the pond. We each have a basket holding several jars, the weight of them tugging at my arms.

We dig silently, hole after hole, burying demon after demon, returning inside with our jars empty, and our hearts lighter.

'Hazel!' Mama screams, her voice rising above the crowd in the airport. Grant and I are each holding a sign with my parents' names on it – I wrote mine in Arabic to make it stand out. But I drop it now and rush through the crowd, launching myself at my parents, almost knocking them to the floor.

'Let me look at you!' Mama says, wrapping her hands on either side of my face and I know with certainty they would never have left me forever.

'Your hands are cold!' I say, feigning protest, but I place mine on her wrists so she knows I don't want her to let go.

'You've grown!' Dad says, eyes welling up with tears. 'And your clothes, they're . . .'

'Grant dressed me,' I say, grinning. We went to a charity shop and she taught me how to find cool old clothes. I'm kind of disappointed I'll have to wear a uniform next week, because Ruby would love some of my new outfits.

I bought lots of T-shirts, especially, because I don't need to hide my hands any more. But England is getting colder now so I'm also wearing a denim jacket, which I painted a white rabbit on, for luck, and a pair of tartan trousers like Grant's.

Mama and Dad turn to Grant now that she's managed to catch up with us. Mama introduces herself nervously, before pulling me aside to let her speak with Dad. They pull each other into a fierce hug, and I hear Grant whisper, 'I'm so happy you're here.'

On the way home Dad sits in the front to catch up with Grant, and I sit in the back with Mama, telling her all about England and the new things I've discovered since moving here.

'So tonight we're eating something called toad in the hole,' I say, as we pull up to Grant's gingerbread house. 'But don't worry, it's not an *actual* toad,' I assure her.

For some reason they all laugh at this, and it's nice to hear my family's joyful voices replacing the fireflies' silky whispers.

CHAPTER 37

'Well done, Ezra and Akin,' says Ms Basra as everyone claps. They've just done their final presentation, where they took it in turns to read their story and explained how they decided to interpret them. It's the first week of the *actual* school year now, and we'll be doing fairy tales all term. Ms Basra asked those of us who were at summer school to present our stories as a way to introduce the topic to everyone else. There are lots more people in the class now, lots more people for me to get to know.

At the end of term we're going to put our stories together in an anthology, and Ms even asked *me* to be the illustrator after I showed her my painting of the firefly forest.

Ezra and Akin's theme was 'prince' so they decided to do a spin on 'Cinderella'. Instead of marrying the prince, she discovers he's actually an alien cyborg planning to destroy the village. It's only when she reveals the prince for who he really is, in front of everyone at the ball, that she's free from her stepmother and stepsisters, and becomes a secret agent.

'She's good at listening,' Akin explained. 'Because she's spent her whole life blending in to the background.'

'And when she opens up her spy agency, her animal friends help her because they can sneak around too,' continued Ezra.

'Also, because she worked in a big house, she knows where all of the secret passages are. So basically, her whole life is set up for her to become a spy,' finished Akin, and you can tell they're both proud. It's a really cool idea.

'I absolutely *love* this,' Ms Basra says. 'The way you've cleverly made it about Cinderella but still focused on your theme. And I love that you've thought about the skills she would have grown up with and used them in an interesting way. Perhaps she could have lots of spy gadgets that look like cleaning products?'

'Miss, that's a good idea!' says Akin, and he nudges Ezra as they write that down.

They chat for a while longer about their ideas, and I take a deep breath and think of mine and Ruby's. I'm a little nervous after seeing Ezra and Akin's idea because it's cool and catchy, and I think ours might be a bit messy and complicated. Plus there are a lot more people to present to.

But we couldn't just ignore the fireflies, and the witch, and the headless horseman and the wolf, could we? So when we stand up and tell our story, it's *my* story we're telling.

As we did with our mood board, we bring in something wild to accompany our story: my jar of luck with the yellow polka-dot lid, which has turned into a bit of a bug terrarium. The other students in our class shuffle in their seats to look closer, and I can tell they're interested already.

I also have my forest painting, to 'help set the mood', as Ruby said to convince me to show it to everyone.

We talk about a young girl who is forced to fight her demons in the woods. The demons shift into her fears and eat her worries, growing stronger with them. But the trees protect her and guide her home each time, and with their help she learns to fight. She has other help too, her talismans: a frog, a snail shell and a ladybird.

And eventually, the demons grow weaker, and weaker, until they shrink to the size of ants.

'And what fairy-tale inspirations did you use?' Ms Basra finally asks. It's hard to tell whether she likes our story or not, because she looks very serious when she speaks to us, and the room has gone quiet. I can't even hear everyone else breathing now, because all I hear is the beat, beat, beat of my heart which sounds like it's coming from behind my ears.

Ruby glances at me, and she points at herself, asking if I want her to answer. But I shake my head.

'We didn't pick one fairy tale,' I say, training my eyes on the clock at the back of the room. It's quarter to ten. In fifteen minutes the bell will ring for a short break, followed by biology. I'm most excited about biology because of the bugs and flowers, but right now I focus on my answer to Ms Basra. 'We used fairy-tale t-tropes, which means a theme that crops up in them, such as the breadcrumb trail, like in Hansel and Gretel, except ours has ants and mushrooms. We also used the rule of threes, and lucky objects and creatures which were enchantments to fight the curse. The story focuses on a witch, which was our theme, but there are other creatures too: a wolf and a horseman. The wolf threatens to eat the witch, like in Little Red Riding Hood, and the main character gets sent on her quest as punishment for stealing fruit, like in Rapunzel.'

I take a deep breath, gathering the words I need for the next bit of the presentation and continue.

'But even though we've used those inspirations, our twist is that, unlike the fairy tales we're used to reading, ours never ends. Because you don't always get a happy ending, but maybe what you get instead is the armour to fight. That's our moral too.'

As I say this last bit, I hold up the jar – my armour.

Ms Basra is silent for a moment, like she's actually chewing our words over, tasting them, and swallowing them. And then, after a moment, she grins wide.

'Wow,' she says. 'I'm so impressed with what you've done.' She starts clapping and the rest of the class follows. Next to us, on the other side of Ms Basra are Ezra and Akin. They both give us a thumbs up and grin. As the claps die down and the room falls silent again, Ms Basra turns to us. 'I promise this is my last question. Going back to your original character of the witch. What do you think you've learned about them?'

'That witches are misunderstood,' I say quickly, confidently. 'And they're not *bad* like the ones in the stories that inspired us.' I think of Grant, and how I thought *she* was bad because of the jars she had hidden and her secrets, but it was because I didn't know her full story. And I guess, in some ways, what I did was bad: taking Amélie, not showing up home on time, but someone who saw me act that way wouldn't know *my* full story. 'That's why the witch looks like the character that goes into the firefly forest. Because, really, they're the same.'

Ms Basra nods and nods as I speak, and while she goes to get a 'surprise' for us, Ruby pats me on the shoulder and whispers that I was great. Even though she was confident at summer school, she seems much more nervous with lots more people in our class. But it's OK, because she has me, and together we can do anything.

'Before the bell rings, I'd love to introduce you to your four library assistants,' Ms Basra says, passing us each a shiny badge shaped like an open book. We're meant to wear it on our blazers, so everyone can see.

She explains that we have special access to the library at break times (which usually only the older students are allowed), and that we'll be working with her to set up events at school.

I turn to Ruby excitedly and she seems even happier than I am about it. By the time we sit down for our next lesson, I'm completely relaxed, and by the time Ruby and I walk home together, we're chatting away about all of the exciting things that happened at school.

When we walk through the door Grant is there with my parents. They're standing in the kitchen with a giant pizza and lots of fizzy drinks and snacks for me and Ruby. Her parents are there too, and they're all throwing us a little party to celebrate the end of our first week at secondary school.

And in that moment, all of the scary newness of this place feels familiar and comforting. I told Mama and Dad about the fireflies too, the first night they arrived. So now, if the fireflies come back, I have my parents, Grant *and* my best friend to help me fight them. What's more, Grant said that when I'm ready, if I ever need it, I can go with her to Little Nook Mental Health Centre to speak to a professional. They let me keep my jar of luck, because they know it helps, and each week Grant tells me about the demons she fights, before we bury them in the garden together. That way I know I'm not the only one.

After everything I've been through, I think I can now start to call this place home.

...EVER AFTER

The girl was visited by the fireflies again, as she had expected. They took her into their forest, which was crumbling and ashen. But if you know anything about trees, you'll know that their hearts and souls exist beneath the ground, in the roots that dig deep and take hold.

So as the girl stepped along the broken paths and half-burned trees, she knew their wounds would heal. And on the floor she could see a cluster of wildflowers surrounding the wounded trees like a protective army. Their colours were so vivid, and their petals so plentiful, that they shone brighter than the fireflies that lived within.

AUTHOR'S NOTE AND RESOURCES

OCD is short for Obsessive Compulsive Disorder, and it makes you have the same thoughts over and over, which makes you want to repeat the same tasks, over and over, until the thought goes away.

I first noticed I had OCD when I was eight or nine – the same age as some of you reading this book. Mine was different to Hazel's fireflies, but it made me have similar feelings to her:

I felt OUT OF CONTROL when the thoughts happened making me need to complete the tasks the way Hazel completes her quest.

I felt RELIEVED when I finished the task, but not for very long because another thought and task would appear in my mind soon after.

I felt SCARED about someone finding out because they

would think it was strange and stop me from doing the tasks, which would make me feel really bad.

I felt TIRED because having to do the tasks, like Hazel's quest, took up lots of energy, and it made it difficult to focus on anything else.

But I felt BETTER when I told someone about it, and they understood how I was feeling and helped me fight the OCD.

Sometimes the OCD comes back - the way the fireflies return to Hazel – but slowly, with the help of people who care about me and professionals who understand, I build up more tools to fight it.

If you're ever feeling alone with your thoughts, it can help to share them with someone, no matter how strange or silly they seem. Maybe start with a guardian, a teacher, or a trusted friend.

And for guardians of children dealing with OCD here are a list of resources to help:

- https://childmind.org/guide/quick-guide-to-obsessive-compulsive-disorder-ocd/
- https://kidshealth.org/en/parents/ocd.html
- https://www.anxietyuk.org.uk/wp-content/uploads/2020/10/Helpling-your-child-with-Obsessive-Compulsive-Disorder.pdf
- https://ocdyouth.org

WITH THANKS TO ...

Claire Wilson

Sarah Levison

Olivia Adams

Laura Bird

Safae El-Ouahabi

Lucy Courtenay

Susila Baybars

Aleena Hasan

Sam Coates

Jasveen Bansal

Samara Iqbal

Pippa Poole

Seema Mitra

And to the other lovely people who had a hand in this book, including booksellers, educators, and fellow authors for your continued support.

Read on for a
sneak peek of

A
Pocketful
of
Stars

Chapter 1

Mum always turns everything into a game. Even boring days out to the theatre.

'When the play starts,' Mum says, 'count the number of times the cast say Rapunzel's name. Apparently they say it seven times in the first seven minutes!' She pauses, looking between me and my best friend Elle. We glance at each other and frown. 'Seven!' Mum repeats, like this should mean something to us. 'The witching number?' She looks disappointed. 'Oh, never mind.'

I can't help but laugh. Mum's games don't always make sense, because her brain works in mysterious ways.

We're at a coffee shop next door to the theatre, having cake and hot chocolate while we wait to watch an afternoon performance of *Rapunzel*.

'Fine, you think of a better game to play while we watch,'

she says, chucking her napkin at me, grinning.

'We could just watch the play?' I offer.

Mum snorts, shaking her head. 'Boring.'

'OK, fine.' I think for a moment. 'How about we count the number of times the cast says "hair"?' I suggest. 'Isn't that what the story is about?'

It's Mum's turn to laugh. '*Rapunzel* isn't about hair!' she says. 'I've never heard something so ridiculous. It's about freedom, and independence, and exploring the world.'

While Mum talks, I look up a line from the story on my phone and read it out, smirking. '"Rapunzel, Rapunzel, let down thy hair." You have to admit, Mum, it does seem to be about hair . . .'

'Cheeky,' Mum says, taking a sip of her coffee. 'Anyway, what about you, Elle, what do you think we should count?'

Elle, who's been watching us talk back and forth like a referee at a tennis match, chimes in. 'We've been doing Shakespeare at school this year, and apparently whenever anyone performs *Macbeth*, it's bad luck to say his name in the theatre before the play!'

Mum looks genuinely interested. 'Yes, I have heard this! But also, did you know . . .' And soon enough Mum and Elle have launched into a conversation about different traditions in the theatre – something I could never talk about.

Elle's like a chameleon, she always knows what to say. She changes personalities depending on who she's around and can talk to just about anyone, like Mum. I'm just a plain old lizard, darting into the corner of every room I enter.

While they talk, I get distracted by the countdown on my phone. *Fifteen minutes.*

That's when tickets to the biggest video gaming convention of the year are released. Dad promised he would go with me if I could get us both tickets. I've been saving up my birthday money for it.

The thing is, they can sometimes sell out in minutes, so you have to be quick.

'Hurry up, Safiya!' Mum calls. I look up and find her at the door of the coffee shop tapping her feet, impatient to leave.

Mum and I look so similar we could almost be twins, apart from our hair and my glasses. We both have olive skin and brown eyes. Except Mum has black curls that float down her back, whereas my hair hangs by my waist in limp waves.

'Mum, the play doesn't start for another half-hour,' I protest. Secretly I want to stay here long enough to buy the tickets before we go inside. But if I tell Mum that she won't understand.

'I want to find our seats early, get comfortable!'

'And that takes half an hour?'

Mum sighs, opens her mouth to retort, and then storms out of the coffee shop.

I can't help but roll my eyes. Mum can be so hot and cold sometimes, like a sunny winter's day. Things can be going really well, then suddenly everything changes.

The truth is, even though Mum and I look alike, we're not very similar in other ways. Often it's like we're on different pages of the same book, always just missing each other as the page turns.

'Come on, Saff,' Elle says, reaching for my hand. She's used to mine and Mum's bickering now.

When we get into the theatre foyer it's packed, and I walk with Elle until we find Mum outside the hall, tickets in hand. She hasn't seen us yet.

Elle says she's going to pop to the toilets quickly so I stop, for a moment, and watch Mum standing there alone. Her eyes are far away, like they're in a different world entirely. Mum's been so intense about this show, more than I've ever seen her before. You'd think we were going to the West End, not the local theatre in our tiny town.

A member of staff approaches her and Mum's eyes focus again. 'No thank you,' she says when the woman asks if she needs any help. 'I'm just waiting for my daughter and her friend.' Then she comments on how lovely the woman's earrings are and her face lights up as she tells Mum that she made them herself. Soon enough they're in a full-blown conversation about jewellery-making, even though Mum knows nothing about it.

Mum's good at talking to people, being a lawyer. She

knows exactly what to say at all times. I'm different. I only know how to express myself in video games. Instead of words, I use spells and incantations.

Once the woman leaves, Mum's face falls into a frown. She checks her watch and glances anxiously across the foyer, just as Elle taps me on the shoulder. Then Mum sees us. Except she sees Elle before me, because she stands out way more than I do, with her bright red mane like a beacon of light.

'There you are!' Mum says, relieved, but I can hear the annoyance in her voice too.

I check the time. Five minutes until the convention tickets are released.

'I'm just going to the toilet!' I say. 'Be back in a second.'

Mum lets out a noise that sounds like a monster is living inside her. She hands me my ticket, barely looking at me now. 'You'll have to find your seat alone,' she warns, like I'm five years old, and not thirteen.

Once Mum and Elle have disappeared inside the hall I run back outside the theatre and into the coffee shop again, where they have Wi-Fi. I log in to my account and watch the countdown.

Two minutes.

'Did you want a drink?' the person behind the counter asks.

I stare at him blankly.

'You're not really supposed to be in here without a

drink,' he clarifies, a little more sternly.

I hate being told off.

My eyes dart between the coffee-shop guy and the countdown on my phone, and I panic, frozen. I try to open my mouth but it's like it's glued shut. I am not good under pressure with strangers. So I just shake my head and run back out on to the street.

Stupid, Saff, I think, feeling embarrassed. If Mum or Elle were here they would have been able to talk to him and say, 'Yes, just an orange juice please,' and buy the tickets to the gaming convention, and everything would be fine.

Instead I stand on the street for fifteen minutes, where the Wi-Fi doesn't work, and there's hardly any signal. I try to load the page over and over, until all the tickets have sold out and the page shows a big sad smiley face with a pop-up bubble that says 'Maybe next year'.

To make everything worse, by the time I get back to the theatre the play's already started. Mum's going to be furious!

I slip into my seat after stepping on about five people's toes, almost knocking a drink out of someone's hand, and getting a few tuts from older men and women. And when I'm finally in my seat I shrink so low I'm surprised I haven't morphed into a turtle, hiding inside its shell . . .